Praise for <u>Anita of Rancho del Mar</u>

"*Anita of Rancho del Mar* is a sensitively written story about a young girl's life in Alta California during the 1830s. The author sympathetically yet honestly deals with the myriad problems that plagued the rancho owners during Alta California's tumultous history, including boundaries, finances, unstable government, *bandidos,* etc. At the same time the reader gets an insight into the culture of the *Gente de Razón.* This book would make an excellent contribution to a period that has too often been heavily romanticized. It not only has local appeal because of its setting in Ventura County, but has appeal to children throughout the country."

—*Judith P. Triem*
Historian; author, <u>Ventura County, Land of Good Fortune</u>

"A delightfully exciting story! Anita is an especially well drawn character. Pre-teens and early teenage girls will identify with her.

"Not only does this story have educational applications in the study of California history; it will also have wide appeal to all who enjoy a 'good story.'"

—*Mavis Barnhill*
Curriculum Library, Ventura Unified School District

"I truly liked this book! I found the description of rancho life very faithful to reality. It has great possibilities in the children's literature field. There is a crying need for this kind of supplementary reading."

—*Yetive Hendricks*
Publications Committee,
Ventura County Museum of History and Art

"A delightful story that fills a real vacuum in the grammar school curriculum."

—*Patricia Clark*
Editor, Museum Publications,
Ventura County Museum of History and Art

ANITA
OF RANCHO DEL MAR

by
Elaine F. O'Brien

Illustrated by
Francine Rudesill

FITHIAN PRESS ❦ SANTA BARBARA, CALIFORNIA ❦ 1991

LIBRARY OF CONGRESS CATALOGING-IN-PUBLICATION DATA
O'Brien, Elaine F., 1920–
    Anita of Rancho Del Mar / Elaine F. O'Brien ; illustrated by Francine Rudesill
    p.   cm.
    Summary: Depicts life on a Spanish land-grant ranch in California in the 1830s
    through the adventures of young Anita and the Lorenzana family.
    ISBN: O-931832-79-9
    [1. California--Fiction. 2. Ranch life--Fiction.]
    I. Rudesill, Francine, ill. II. Title.
    PZ7.01268An   1991
    [Fic]--dc20   90-19711
                                     CIP
                                     AC

CONTENTS

Acknowledgment
The author wishes to give special thanks to the docents
of the Ventura County Museum of History and Art for
their help and encouragement.
Chapter three, "On the Sespe," originally appeared in
California Historian, *a publication of the Conference of*
California Historical Societies, Volume 37, Number 3,
April, 1991.

The Missions of
California

† San Francisco Solano
San Rafael †
San Francisco
Santa Clara † † San Jose
Monterey Bay San Juan Bautista †
Monterey †
San Carlos Borromeo † † Soledad
† San Antonio de Padua
† San Miguel
† San Luis Obispo
La Purisima Concepción † † Santa Inez
† Santa Barbara
† San Buenaventura
San Miguel I. † San Fernando †
Santa Rosa I. Santa Cruz I. † Los Angeles San Bernardino
Channel Islands † San Gabriel
Santa Barbara I. Santa Catalina I. † San Juan Capistrano
San Clemente I. † San Luis Rey
† San Diego

Sierra Nevada
Cajon Pass
Colorado River

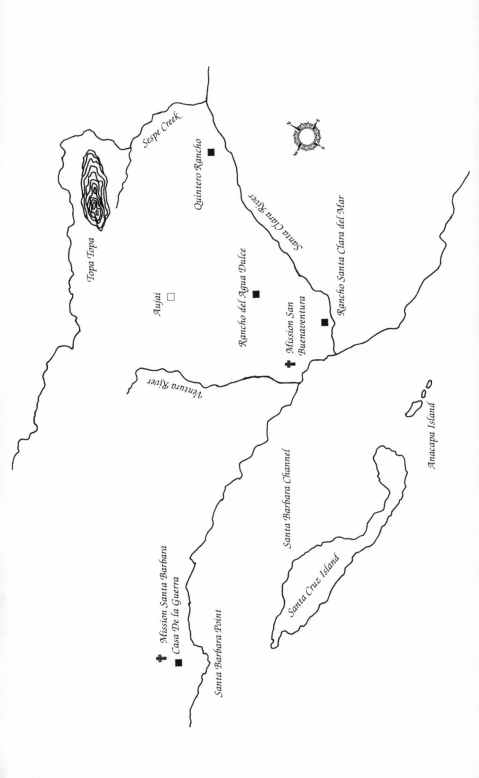

For Caitlin Elizabeth

SILVER SPURS

A **thin gray ribbon** of smoke reared up from the valley floor like an angry cobra ready to strike. Grassfire! Two riders, a girl of twelve and a boy thirteen, wheeled their ponies off the river trail and galloped in a headlong race across the tinder dry grass to the undulating gray menace. With hearts pounding they swung down from their saddles, snatched their water flasks and emptied the contents on the smoldering gray ash.

"Just in time." The girl took a long deep breath. Her name was Ana María Magdalena Dolores Lorenzana y Toral, but her father called her Anita. She tipped back her broad-brimmed sombrero and brushed a black curl out of her dark eyes. "That fire could have burned all the grass on our *rancho*. Lucky there's no wind today. Who would be stupid enough to leave a live campfire?"

"City people from Mexico, probably," said her brother Tonio. "No California *ranchero* would ride away from a smoking fire." His booted feet kicked the warm ashes and stamped out a glowing ember. He wiped his forehead with his white handkerchief. His alert green eyes watched a distant cloud of yellow dust moving north toward the rocky peak of Topa Topa.

"They camped here on our land last night. Strange. They didn't come to the ranch house." Anita tied her water flask to her pony's saddle. Her cheeks felt warm from the headlong gallop. She shook out her flowered skirt and tucked in her round-necked blouse at the waist as she walked around the campsite. Her small foot stepped on something soft and flat. She reached down and picked up a finely tooled leather pocket case half hidden in the dust. "Somebody dropped this."

"Open it up. Let's see what's inside. Maybe we can find out who camped here." Tonio secured his water flask to his saddle with a leather strap and walked over to his sister.

"It's a piece of heavy folded paper. Looks like a map with pictures."

"Let me see." Tonio unfolded the ink-smudged sheet. "It is a map."

Anita peered over his elbow. "Look, there's the ocean, a river, hills and some trees. It's not finished though."

"It's a *diseño* of our land grant, Rancho Santa Clara del Mar. That's what this is. Look, right here. There's Topa Topa Mountain and our ranch house near the ocean." Tonio frowned and his tanned face became serious. "Why would someone be making a map of our *rancho*? We had better show this to Father right away."

"He'll be angry. We're not supposed to ride so far from the ranch house."

"Well, we had to put out the fire, didn't we?"

Anita glanced across the valley. "They're coming back."

Two riders emerged from the distant dust cloud and began backtracking toward the campsite. Bending their heads low, they leaned from one side of their saddles to the other, searching the ground on either side of their trail.

Tonio buttoned the case safely in his jacket pocket. "Let's get away from here, but not too fast. We don't want them to suspect anything. Their horses can overtake our ponies."

The two young *rancheros* mounted quickly and turned westward toward the ocean and home. The ponies loped along the river trail at a good pace. After riding a quarter of a mile, Anita looked over her shoulder. The strangers had reached the dead fire and were searching the campsite. She saw one raise his arm and point to Tonio and herself. The strangers spurred their horses and galloped in pursuit.

"Hurry! They're following us," Anita shouted in alarm. Her heart beat fast and a lump of cold fear rose in her throat. She kicked her heels into her pony's sides and urged him to a full gallop. Tonio followed close behind. They raced toward home pursued by the strangers.

Tonio's keen eyes picked out a flurry of dust on the trail ahead. "More riders. Let's hope they're our *vaqueros*." He stared hard into the distance and yelled, "It's Father and the twins!"

"They see us!"

Don José, Enrique and Fernando galloped forward three abreast and blocked the trail. They faced toward the strangers while Anita and Tonio rode past as fast as their ponies could carry them. Outnumbered, the strangers gave up the chase, turned around, and galloped back toward the mountains.

Anita and Tonio pulled up their ponies to a stop and waited until their father and twin brothers joined them. Don José's green eyes blazed at Anita and Tonio from under his broad-brimmed hat. "Lucky for you that we came out to find you. Why did you disobey me?" He listened to Anita's explanation with stern attention. He examined the *diseño* with a sober face and carefully put it back in the case. His expression softened as he looked at Anita's troubled face. "You and Tonio did the right thing. You both used good judgment. Sometimes rules must be broken. Let's not say anything to anyone about this until after the fiesta."

Preparations for Doña Francisca's party began before dawn the next day. The ranch house hummed with activity as everyone worked to make the party a success. Noise and laughter and the smell of good things cooking penetrated every corner of the house and courtyard. Don José had invited guests from far and near to attend a fiesta in honor of his wife's birthday, a birthday the family would never forget.

Anita walked out through the kitchen doorway. In her arms she held a wooden box of tallow candles. She paused for a moment in the shade of the ranch house porch and set the wooden box down on a bench. She inhaled the fragrant perfume of the climbing roses and admired the pots of flowering plants that splashed the porch with brilliant colors. She sat down to watch the *vaqueros* working at the barbecue in the corner of the walled courtyard. Anita would rather have been riding her pony, but everyone was busy. She was not allowed to ride off alone. Fierce grizzlies hid in the brush near the cattle grazing on the hills.

Sometimes outlaws traveled north along the river trail. As she sat on the bench in the shade, she thought about her new satin dancing slippers, and tapped her feet in time to the *fandango* music playing inside her head. She listened to the soft pitty-pitty-pat as the maid servants patted out the *masa* between their hands making *tortillas* in the shade of the *ramada*. In the kitchen, knives clattered as the cook and her helper chopped vegetables for the *salsa*. The spicy smell of onions, tomatoes and *cilantro* escaped through the doorway to the porch, where the breeze captured the tantalizing aroma and carried it across the courtyard. Anita heard the hiss and spatter of melting suet as the quarters of beef and lamb cooked slowly over the glowing coals. Two strong *vaqueros* leaned over the barbecue and turned the heavy pieces of meat over and over on the grill.

Tonio walked around the side of the house and stepped on the porch. He sat down beside his sister, sniffed the air with satisfaction, and said, *"Barbacoa."* Two years ago he and Anita had often been mistaken for twins with their dark curly hair, long Lorenzana noses and dimples in their cheeks when they smiled, which was often. In the last year, however, Tonio had grown two inches and had developed new muscles in his shoulders and chest.

He leaned toward his sister and whispered, "Did Father tell Mother about the two strangers and that leather case we found yesterday?"

"No, he didn't want to spoil her birthday." Anita stood up and picked some candles out of the box. She set each one firmly in the iron candle holders nailed to the big timbers that braced the second floor balcony overhead. "M-m-m. You smell nice, Tonio. What have you been doing?"

"I squeezed three baskets of oranges and one of lemons for Mother's special *refresco*. I still have another batch to do." He looked around for his eldest brother. "Where's Lorenzo?"

Anita peeked inside the large red clay *ollas* hanging at both ends of the porch to make sure each was filled with fresh cool drinking water. "He's brushing out his best suit and polishing the silver buttons on his trousers."

"Polishing his buttons? They're so shiny now you can see your face in them. They're like mirrors. Who's coming tonight anyway?"

"Cecelia Vargas is coming from Santa Barbara with her mother and brothers and a couple of the de la Guerras, also Carmen Garza and her family from Rancho San Marco. Did you know that Father has hired an orchestra from Santa Barbara? The army sergeant and six soldiers from the San Buenaventura *cuartel* are coming. So is that American, Captain Biddle, who is buying hides from us. Some of his sailors will be here. By the way, the captain is giving us payment in gold."

"Gold? Not silver? That's unusual. He must need those hides pretty bad. He has to have a full hold before he can sail back to Boston." Tonio walked to the *olla* and took a drink of water. "I haven't seen Enrique and Fernando all day. Where are they?"

"The twins are working with the men. They're making corrals out of brush to hold the oxen and horses of our guests," replied his sister. Anita always knew where everyone was and what they were doing.

"Where's María Isabel?"

"Upstairs. She's fixing her hair."

Their sixteen-year-old sister had gathered flowers from the garden early that morning with Tía Luisa. She carefully arranged large bouquets in all the rooms. "She's sitting before the mirror trying on different hair ribbons for the best effect," said Anita. María Isabel was beautiful and she knew it. Most of the young men from Santa Barbara to San Fernando were half in love with her.

Tonio smiled. "There'll be at least six calf-eyed *rancheros* hanging around her tonight, each one asking her to dance."

At that moment they heard the clippity-clop of hoofs as a horse loped along the path outside the courtyard wall. They turned their heads toward the open gateway.

"*Ay, Chihuahua!* What a beautiful horse!" exclaimed Tonio. "Who is the rider?"

"He's a stranger," said his sister. "I never saw him before."

Across the walled courtyard a tall, well-dressed man on a magnificent black horse entered through the gateway, dismounted, and approached the shaded porch of the ranch house. "Good afternoon. May I have a drink of water?" he asked politely. Anita hurried to the *olla* and poured out a drink of cool water. "Thank you," said the man.

"Welcome to Rancho del Mar, *señor*," said Tonio, remembering his manners.

Don José heard the strange voice and came out through the *sala* door. "Welcome. *Mi casa es suya.* (My house is yours.) I am José Lorenzana."

"Thank you. My name is Ramón Gutiérrez de Navarre. I have been traveling for many weeks from Mexico. I am on my way north to Monterey."

"You must be tired from such a long journey," said Don José courteously. "Come inside the house where it is cool. You may rest until our fiesta begins this evening. You are welcome to stay."

"Thank you very much, *señor*. I seem to have come at the right time," answered Don Ramón. The silver spurs on his soft leather boots jingled musically across the porch. Tonio went off to call a *vaquero* who would feed and water the black horse in the corral. Anita wondered what María Isabel would think of this handsome stranger from Mexico. She went inside to tell Doña Francisca about the interesting guest. "Mother, he has such elegant manners! He walks like a duke from old Spain."

"How would you know how a duke walks," scoffed her brother as he entered the *sala*. "You've never seen one."

"Well, he walks the way I think a duke would walk," replied Anita.

"Hush, children," said Doña Francisca in her gentle voice. "Tonio, you might learn some manners from him."

An hour later, dressed in her best red silk dress, Anita came out on the second floor balcony and looked over the railing. The sun hung low in the sky. The sweating *vaqueros* were still turning meat on the hot and smoking barbecue. The breeze that suddenly blew in from the sea brought a welcome wave of cool air.

She turned to the east, up the valley. Two dust clouds appeared in the distance. Here come the guests from Somis and Saticoy, she said to herself. Those from San Fernando must have been delayed. They may not arrive before sunset.

There was no cloud of dust coming from the neighboring *rancho* to the northeast. Relations between the Lorenzanas of Rancho del Mar and the Valencias of Rancho del Agua Dulce were strained. While the families treated each other politely, a serious boundary dispute smoldered under a surface of cool civility.

Guests from other *ranchos* to the southeast and northwest were also making their way along the winding dusty trails that led to Rancho Santa Clara del Mar, or as the

Lorenzanas called it, Rancho del Mar. Little children and babies and elderly ladies traveled in the old-fashioned two-wheeled *carretas,* sitting on sheepskins and soft down pillows. The *carretas* creaked and lurched along on their huge wooden wheels, drawn by slow moving oxen. The tops were arched over with bleached cotton cloth to shade the passengers from the hot sun. Riders looped their lariats around the hubs of the wheels to help the oxen pull the carts over the rough or steep places on the road. Behind the *carretas* rode family groups on horseback. Often a woman sat on the saddle in front of a man who held the reins and guided the horse. Other men and women rode alone on their favorite horses. All the guests were dressed in their finest clothes. The women wore colorful silk dresses with full skirts and the men wore tight fitting dark jackets and white shirts. A line of bright silver buttons decorated the outside seams of their trousers. Anita could almost hear the families laughing and singing as they rode toward Rancho del Mar.

Anita turned away from the railing and entered the room where her father and Captain Biddle were talking. She wanted Don José to see her new satin slippers. Waiting politely, she stood by the closed connecting door that led to Don Ramón's room. He's been sleeping a long time, she thought. Then she heard a faint rustle and a board creak on the other side of the door. Someone was listening. She stood still and breathed quietly. Don José and the bearded sea captain struck a deal to exchange gold and trade goods for steer hides. The heavy coins clinked as her father dropped them into a leather pouch. He tied the top of the pouch and dropped it with a thud into the trunk at the foot of the bed.

"I'll send this to the de la Guerras' strong room in Santa

Barbara for safekeeping." Don José locked the trunk. "I can pay some bills and buy silks and velvets for my wife and tools for the ranch. Come, let us go down to the courtyard. The orchestra is tuning up." Don José ushered Captain Biddle to the balcony, smiled at his daughter, and nodded his approval of the new satin slippers.

Her father and the sea captain walked downstairs. Anita remained by the door without moving. Then she heard a board creak again and the faint sounds of someone pulling on boots. Without making a sound, she walked across the floor and entered her own room through the connecting door on the opposite side. She looked in the mirror, adjusted a wayward curl, and went outside through the balcony door. She stood by the railing. In the fading light she could see the peak above Mugu Lagoon. I'm glad we live here, she thought.

Four large bedrooms opened out on the long balcony that offered a full view of the courtyard, the Santa Clara River, and the grassy slopes of the valley. There were no windows or doors on the north side of the house. Thick *adobe* brick walls covered with brown plaster kept the rooms cool in summer and warm in winter. The house itself formed one side of the rectangle that composed the large courtyard. The other three sides were high walls of plastered *adobe* brick topped with red tiles. When the gate in the south wall was closed at night, foxes and coyotes could not get in to steal the chickens, and wild cattle could not blunder in to munch on Doña Francisca's flowers.

Don Ramón left his room and joined Anita on the balcony. "You have an unusual house," he remarked. "There are not many two-story homes in California."

"We have a good view of the fiesta from here," said Anita.

Side by side they looked at the scene below. Long tables were set up in the courtyard laden with platters of fruit, baskets of freshly made *tortillas*, big bowls of *frijoles*, more platters piled high with mouth-watering slices of barbecued beef and lamb, and small bowls of *chile salsa*. The maids arranged plates of honey cakes and dishes of a delicious custard called *flan* side by side with baskets of figs, dried apricots, almonds, and pumpkin candy from the Mission.

"Won't you come downstairs and join us?" Anita sensed something watchful and wary about this quiet man with the elegant manners. Don Ramón motioned for her to precede him down the stairs.

At the foot of the stairway, Don Ramón picked a rose from the vine growing by the porch and placed it in his lapel. He cast a sharp glance at the five American sailors and looked long and hard at the sergeant and the soldiers from the *cuartel*.

That's strange, Anita thought. Why is he staring at the soldiers and sailors? He seems to be counting them.

With easy grace Don Ramón sauntered casually across the hard-packed dirt floor of the courtyard to pay his respects to his host and hostess, to Don José's sister, Tiá Luisa, to the *padre*, and to the other guests. Anita went off to tell her friend, Carmen Garza, about the interesting stranger with the polished manners.

A quartet of musicians walked about playing and singing popular songs. Then the orchestra assembled to play a *jarabe* number. Anita smiled as she watched the guests. Several of the de la Guerra girls tried to teach the young sailors how to dance the *jarabe* with hilarious results. The laughing sailors tripped over their own feet.

Beatriz, the cook, brought out a large tray of sliced fruit

and placed it on a table. A short, red-bearded sailor grabbed her hand and led her through a lively reel. Beatriz laughed and escaped to the kitchen while Tomás, the head *vaquero*, scowled at the sailor from the doorway. The redbearded sailor began to play magic tricks with the children. He pulled pennies out of their ears and curls. They crowded around him, saying, "Me! Me!" "Me next, Barbaroja!" "No, me!"

The Americans don't understand a word of Spanish, Anita thought, but they're having a good time anyway. She smoothed out her red silk skirt and tapped her feet in their black satin slippers.

At intermission, while the orchestra rested their fingers and ate barbecued beef, the American sailors stood up in the center of the courtyard. One produced a whistle from his pocket and played a tune while his shipmates danced a lively hornpipe. The guests cheered, whistled shrilly through their teeth, and beat time. Then one young blond, blue-eyed sailor borrowed a violin. He played and sang about his "Bonita far over the sea." Anita did not understand the English words he sang, but she understood the meaning. When the song ended another sailor grabbed five oranges and began juggling them. The small children cheered, *"Viva! Viva!"*

Now the soldiers took a turn to show what they could do. They laid six sharp swords on the ground with the cutting edges of the blades facing up. The music started slowly as the soldiers stepped back and forth among the blades. Then the musicians played faster and faster. The soldiers' feet moved faster and faster above the blades. Their feet never touched the sharp edges. The music stopped suddenly with a single heavy drum beat. The soldiers bowed as the guests clapped and whistled.

"Don José! Doña Francisca!" the guests called out. "Sing us a song. Sing us a song." Someone pressed a guitar into Don José's hands. He led his wife to the center of the courtyard. With clear musical voices, they sang an old love song from long ago in Mexico, "*Amor, amor, amor,* I'll love you forever."

After that the orchestra tuned up for a lively *fandango*. Guests were choosing partners and lining up opposite each other. Don Ramón had been conversing quietly on the porch bench with Tía Luisa and the *padre*. He stood up and moved gracefully across the courtyard, bowed before Doña Francisca, and said, "May I have your permission to dance with your daughter, *señora*?"

Doña Francisca smiled. "Of course, *señor*."

María Isabel fluttered her long eyelashes and peeked out from behind her fan. However, Don Ramón walked right past her and stood before Anita. His eyes twinkled as he made a deep bow and held out his hand to her. María Isabel was furious. Anita looked at her mother. Her mother nodded. Anita danced the whole *fandango* with Don Ramón without making a single misstep. When the dance was over, Don Ramón led Anita back to her chair, made another graceful bow, and gave her the rose from his lapel.

Anita had scarcely sat down in her chair when Carmen's thirteen-year-old brother stood before her, bowed and asked her to dance. The orchestra was playing the music for *el jarabe*. Although Luis was rather shy with girls and did not say much, he was an expert dancer. He had put on a *serape* and jammed a broad-brimmed straw hat firmly on his head. Luis led Anita out on the floor. They stood facing each other tapping their feet to the music. With a nod to Anita from Luis, they started. Anita stood straight, as Tía Luisa had taught her, her head to one side, holding her skirts above the floor so that everyone could see her heels and toes tapping out the rhythm. Luis clasped his hands behind his back, anchoring the corners of the *serape*. He bent over slightly and danced around his partner, his toes and heels like a pair of drumsticks beating a tattoo on the hard ground. What a good dancer, she thought.

When Luis escorted Anita back to her chair, Tía Luisa smiled at them and said, "Well done."

The orchestra played *contra danzas, paso dobles,* more *jarabes* and more *fandangos*. The guests danced until the early morning hours, but a tired, yawning Anita left the party long before that. She entered her own room, ready to fall into bed, but elderly Doña Hermenegilda had arrived there first and lay there gently snoring. Snuggled around her like small puppies were four toddler grandchildren sound asleep. Anita pulled a couple of sheepskins from a chest. Taking an extra pillow and a brown wool blanket, she went into her parents' room. In a dark corner behind a big chair, she curled up under the blanket in a warm, cozy nest of sheepskins and tucked the rose from Don Ramón under her pillow.

In the darkest hour just before dawn, Anita woke from a deep sleep. Someone stood by the big bed, holding a pistol to her father's head. Anita's heart thumped against her ribs.

"Don't make a sound, *señor*. We don't want to wake Doña Francisca, do we?" It was Don Ramón! "Get up and unlock the chest," he whispered. "Keep your hands in front of you."

Helpless before the menacing pistol and fearful for Doña Francisca, Don José opened the chest at the foot of the bed. From under her half-closed eyelids Anita watched the bandit reach inside the chest, feel around, and pull out a package of land title papers. He tossed it back, felt around again, and lifted out the leather bag of gold. He never took his eyes off Don José.

"Good. Now you and I are going outside." Prodded by the pistol, Don José walked out of the bedroom and down the balcony stairs in his bare feet. "Keep going toward the gateway. If you try anything, I'll shoot," said the bandit in a hoarse whisper.

Clutching the blanket around her, Anita crept to the open doorway. She shivered with fear as she watched her father walk across the courtyard. She noticed that Don Ramón had removed his jingling spurs. What could she do to help her father? The soldiers and sailors had left hours ago. Except for a few snores from the guests exhausted by all the dancing and celebrating, no other sound broke the quiet of the night.

She heard Don José whisper in outraged anger, "Is this how you return my hospitality?"

"Look upon it as a loan, Don José. I am sorry to have to do this. Better to lose the gold than the title papers to your ranch."

A silent figure appeared in the gateway. Anita saw a silver hatband glisten in the starlight. The other bandit gagged Don José and tied his hands and feet while Don Ramón held his pistol to the *ranchero's* head. They left him there and raced away. Leather sacks on the horses' feet muffled the sound of galloping hoofs.

Anita ran to the kitchen for a knife while Don José lay helpless on the cold ground. She removed the gag, but could not cut the ropes. Then Tomás arrived to start the cooking fire for Beatriz. "Señor, what happened?" asked the head *vaquero*. Taking out his own knife he quickly cut away the ropes binding Don José.

"We entertained a scorpion among the guests last night," said Don José fuming. "He stung us hard all right. Thank God no one was hurt." He rubbed his wrists and ankles to restore circulation. He looked at his shivering daughter. "Wake your mother and gently tell her what happened. Tell her no one was hurt. Then wake up Beatriz. Tomás, light the cooking fire. I'll wake everyone else. We'll start out after them in half an hour."

Snatching a cold breakfast, the other *rancheros* mounted their horses. Led by Don José and his sons, they rode off in pursuit of the bandits. Dividing themselves into groups, they searched to the east and west along the trail, but Don Ramón Gutiérrez de Navarre and his companion had slipped away without a trace.

After their guests had left, the stunned Lorenzanas gathered together in the *sala*. Don José told the family about the two strangers chasing Anita and Tonio and the incomplete map of Rancho del Mar. Anita looked at her father's drawn face. He thinks someone is trying to do us harm, she said to herself. She listened as he explained their financial crisis without wasting words. There was an undertone of deep anger in his voice.

"We have lost all our hard earned cash. We must start over, round up another thousand head of cattle, spread the hides out to dry, melt down the suet into tallow, and find another buyer. It may take us six months, but we can do it. Until then, no more fiestas, no more buying silks and velvets, or even new ranch tools. We grow plenty of food right here on the ranch, so there is no worry about that. For the present we must use things up, wear them out, and make do with what we have."

His shocked family braced themselves for hard times. Doña Francisca said to her children, "We will keep up appearances, but we won't tell our friends that we are temporarily short of funds. That's family business and very private."

"I can't understand why Don Ramón Gutiérrez— " began María Isabel.

"De Navarre, don't forget," said Lorenzo with an ironic smile.

"De Navarre," repeated María Isabel. "I can't understand why he would rob us. He was certainly raised as a gentleman."

"Not every man who dances well and has elegant manners is honest," observed Tía Luisa.

"All too true," said her brother. "His family may have sent him away from Spain in disgrace. We met men like him in Mexico City. Some charmed wealthy widows into marrying them. Others sank so low that they cheated poor farmers at cards for a few *reales*. They were sometimes killed when found out."

"He must have had help," said Lorenzo. "That hide deal was set up only a few days ago. He knew somehow that Captain Biddle was paying us in gold."

Doña Francisca added, "Somebody near here must have hidden him."

"You're right," said Don José. "We scoured the valley. He got away like an Apache, no sign of him or of the man with him."

"Excuse me, Don José," said a maid servant entering the *sala* . "I found these in Don Ramón's room. He left them behind." She handed Don José a pair of silver spurs.

"He took all our gold and left us a pair of spurs," said Don José, gritting each word through his teeth. He looked at the spurs and said, "I'm going to wear these myself. They'll remind me to be wary of smooth-talking strangers."

Anita walked slowly upstairs to her room. She felt sad and angry at the same time. How could he do that to us, she asked herself. He was so charming. Everyone liked him. Her dark eyes flashed. Don Ramón Gutiérrez de Navarre, indeed! She took out the red rose he had given her and looked at it thoughtfully for a moment. Then she threw it on the floor and crushed it under her heel.

2

MOISÉS

*I*t had rained steadily for three days. Anita hated staying in the house. She went out on the porch and watched the rain drip off the roof and splash on the patio. At least the rain made us stop working so hard and allowed us to rest for a while. We were all so tired, she thought.

Lorenzo came outside and stood beside her. He looked at the wet, gray sky. "Good weather for ducks, but I wanted to go to Santa Barbara today for Cecelia's birthday party."

"They have probably called it off. The roads are bogged down with mud. Oh, Lorenzo, sometimes I think the sun will never shine again."

"It usually does, sooner or later." Her brother smiled.

"Everyone seems to be so touchy."

"That's true. We all have to be so polite to each other and

careful what we say. We'd better stay out of the kitchen, too. Let's go back inside."

A cranky tyrant ruled the kitchen. Beatriz, who was usually so cheerful, was in a very bad temper. The firewood was wet, and Tomás had a hard time lighting the cooking fire for her under the *ramada* out of the rain. The low, brush covered roof kept the smoke from blowing away. Beatriz' eyes were red and watering. Doña Francisca calmed Beatriz by telling her quietly that the family would eat whatever she cooked for the *vaqueros*.

"Make extra *pozole*. We'll manage."

That night, however, when Don José grumbled about eating *pozole* four times in a row, Doña Francisca answered sharply. "Beatriz is doing the best she can. Considering the wet wood and the smoky fire, it's a miracle that we have any hot food to eat at all. I don't know why we can't have an inside kitchen stove. We can afford it. We sold all that wool to the ship's agent last week."

Doña Francisca never spoke like that. The rain is getting on Mother's nerves, Anita thought. She and her brothers and sister became very quiet and were careful to be polite to each other.

"Would you like some fruit?"

"Thank you, but you take some first."

Don José looked down the table at his wife with a soft expression in his green eyes. He said mildly, "You are quite right, Francisca, but we must wait a while longer. As soon as I can, I promise to make arrangements with Padre Ordaz to send us a workman from the Mission."

Doña Francisca did not reply, but six young faces along the table wore six approving smiles.

Beatriz will enjoy using an inside kitchen stove and oven, Anita said to herself. Now the food will be hot when it comes to the table. Three days of rain and pozole made Father know how much we need an indoor stove.

The rainstorm did something else. It brought the whole family together in the sala at the same time. After dinner the Lorenzanas moved away from the table to a charcoal brazier set in the middle of the room. Its copper surface radiated a pleasing warmth. Sheepskins laid on the hard-packed earth in front of the chairs provided a soft place for their feet.

In the dark afternoon while the rain poured down, Don José placed a lighted candle on a small side table and read aloud his favorite chapters from Don Quixote de la Mancha. Anita listened to the famous Spanish novel while she and her sister cut out pieces of cloth for cotton shirts and the boys braided new lariats. That evening, when she sensed her nieces and nephews were bored, Tía Luisa started up some games. They played *alquerque*, Spanish checkers and little bones. Anita liked to play little bones. Everyone sat down on the floor in a circle and tried to throw three apricot pits into a little bowl. The first player who threw all his pits into the bowl won the game. Afterward Don José, Lorenzo and María Isabel sang old songs to the liquid notes of her guitar.

Enrique and Fernando, who spent each day outdoors, felt cramped in the sala. They started a wrestling match on the floor among the sheepskins where Tonio soon joined them.

With a stern look, Don José stopped them quickly. "Do you want to overturn the brazier and set fire to the house?"

Doña Francisca asked a maid to bring in some chocolate in special cups that could be put on the copper cover of the brazier to heat. Tía Luisa invented a new game she called "Family Tree." As they sipped hot chocolate, they took turns telling old stories about grandparents and cousins. The person who could tell the best story won. Don José, Doña Francisca and Tía Luisa told stories about long dead ancestors on both sides of the family in old Mexico. Some of the stories would never be repeated outside the family circle.

Anita liked the one Tía Luisa told about Great-grandfather Vicente who once played cards with the archbishop and won away from him a pair of beautiful white carriage horses that were famous all over the city. The next Sunday Great-grandfather drove his family to Mass at the great cathedral in a carriage drawn by the famous white horses. He sat in the front row near the pulpit. With arms folded he paid close attention and nodded his head in agreement while the archbishop gave a long sermon on the evils of gambling. The archbishop never played cards with Great-grandfather again. With that story Tía Luisa won the game.

With a cup of chocolate in his hand, Don José began to speak in a solemn voice. "I'm glad we are all here together because I have something serious to discuss. As you know, the governor has given a large piece of land to Señor Valencia. Rancho del Agua Dulce is on land that used to belong to Mission San Buenaventura. Señor Valencia and I do not agree about the location of our boundary line.

"Last week when I was in Santa Barbara, my cousin told me that Señor Valencia has petitioned his friend, the governor, for a larger land grant. The piece he wants is part of our Spanish land commission."

Dona Francisca exploded. Her well bred manners concealed a hot temper. "The Spanish Viceroy of Mexico approved and signed our land commission. They can't take our land away from us. It was given to my father for bravery in the service of the King."

"The Mexican government recognizes the legality of the Spanish royal commissions. The title to Rancho del Mar is clear, but who knows what trouble the politicians and their friends can bring down on our heads? We must take care not to make enemies, my dear."

"Tomás says that Señor Valencia knows next to nothing about running a *rancho*," remarked Lorenzo. "He depends upon a man they call El Malo to run it for him."

Anita spoke up. "Beatriz says that El Malo was so cruel to the Chumash working on the *rancho* that they all ran away. She says he has kidnapped other Chumash and forced them to work for him."

Don José's face looked concerned as he warned his children. "Don't have anything to do with that *caporal*. He is a dangerous man."

"I knew the Valencia family in old Mexico," said Tía Luisa with a sniff. "They may call themselves *gente de razón*, but in my opinion, they are pushy upstarts and ignorant, too."

Doña Francisca said with pride, "The first Toral came from Spain with Cortez in 1519. He was an adventurer from a good family. He started up a sugar plantation and sent back to Spain for his wife. She was one of the first Spanish women to come to the New World. One of their sons went out to Manila in the Philippines and did very well in the China trade."

"An adventurer, eh?" Don José hid his worry behind a teasing remark. "Now I know where Anita gets that trait. It comes from your side of the family."

Doña Francisca laughed and got up from her chair. "I think it's time we all went to bed. If the rain stops tomorrow, we'll have a lot of work to do."

When Anita woke the next morning, the rain had

stopped. After breakfast she stepped outside on the porch with Tonio. They saw a break in the clouds where the sun was trying to burst through.

"Let's go riding," said Tonio eager for action.

"I'll be ready in a minute. Have the horses saddled." Anita turned away to rush upstairs.

Don José came out on the porch as they were ready to leave. Three days of rest had removed the tired lines from his face. He held his musket under his arm. "I think I'll shoot a few game birds for dinner." He lowered his voice so that Doña Francisca would not hear. "It will be a change from *pozole*." Then, in a louder voice, he said "Remember, the trail will be muddy so don't tire the horses by galloping them. Check the course of the river for me. I hope our boundaries haven't changed."

As they rode away from the ranch house, Tonio said, "It's great to be outdoors again. If I had to spend one more day, cooped up listening to María Isabel strumming that guitar off key as she worked out the chords, I would go crazy."

"I know how you feel. Everyone was so glad to get out of the house and into the sunlight. Mother, Tía Luisa and María Isabel went right out into the garden after breakfast and began tying up plants and cutting off dead flowers."

As Anita and her brother rode along the river trail, a mile to the east a young Chumash Indian girl crept through the *chaparral* in Conejo Canyon and hurried down the slope toward the river. Gabriela had been running and running. Her lungs were on fire and her feet felt like lead. She clutched her baby firmly and stumbled on. There! There ahead was the River Santa Clara. Must keep going. She panted. Just a little farther.

As a child she had chased rabbits, now she was the rabbit. Behind her she could hear the dogs barking and the harsh voices of the men as they urged their horses on her trail. That evil *caporal,* the head *vaquero,* was the worst. He had beaten her the last time she ran away from Rancho del Agua Dulce. This time she was not going to be caught and taken back to work for that cruel *dueño* and his wife. Her little son must be free.

After the heavy rains the river was in flood. If she could reach the other side, she and the baby would be safe. Her chest heaving as she gulped in air, she stopped on the bank of the swift-running river, pulled an asphalt-coated basket from her back, and placed her baby in it. Gabriela stepped into the icy cold water and pushed the basket in front of her. It floated. She kicked her tired feet to swim farther away from the bank, but she had no strength left.

"Oh, Mother of us all," prayed Gabriela. "Watch over my baby." A swift undertow caught her feet and swept her away. The waters closed over her head. Blackness. She was gone. The basket floated along on the swift current until it bumped gently against the bare branches of a small dead tree caught in a bed of cattails by the river bank.

Off to the west around a bend in the trail, Anita and Tonio rode along in single file, checking the sandbars for stranded cows or calves. They rode along the bank, staying as close to the river as they dared. One never knew when the sandy bank might suddenly give way and horse and rider be swept away by the racing flood waters.

"Look at the size of that tree floating downriver," said Tonio. "It was uprooted by the rain and the wind and washed down from the mountains."

"There's a big rattlesnake on that bare branch." Anita

shivered.

"What a monster! Look at all those rattles! It must be at least seven feet long and as big around as my thigh. It's a black diamondback from the high country."

"He'll never get back to the mountains," said his sister. "He's headed straight for the ocean along with that big tree."

"Look, horses and *vaqueros* up ahead," cried Tonio. "Dogs too. Do you hear them?"

"Yes, it's that *caporal* from Ranch del Agua Dulce. He wears a silver band on his hat. See how it glints in the sunshine? What are they doing on our land anyway?"

"They must be chasing someone or something by the way the dogs are barking. They've seen us. They're calling off the dogs and are turning back to their *rancho* on the other side of the hills." Tonio's green eyes watched the figures disappearing in the distance.

"Tomás doesn't like him. Beatriz says he's evil. Listen, do you hear anything?" Anita turned in her saddle to look along the riverbank. "There it is again. It sounds like a baby."

They walked their horses cautiously along the bank, peering through the underbrush tossed up by the rushing waters. "There," cried Anita. "Right there in the growth of cattails alongside that small dead tree. A baby in a basket. It's close by the bank. Too far out to grab by hand." She dismounted and edged toward the basket.

"Hold it!" Tonio's voice was sharp. "Don't move. There's a rattlesnake on that branch between you and the basket. We'll have to get the snake first, and then the baby."

"Look out! It's moving toward us. Be careful!"

"Don't worry. I've caught a lot of them, but I've never told Mother and don't you tell on me." Tonio got off his horse and searched around in the bushes nearby until he found a straight green branch. He quickly stripped off the leaves and small twigs with his pocketknife to make a long pole. He tied the thin end into a slipknot and tested it carefully. The uneasy horses stamped their hoofs and whinnied. "The rattlesnake has spooked them," he said over his shoulder. "Tie the reins to that small tree over there, and then find a good-sized rock. Stand back."

Anita picked up a heavy rock the size of a large melon and watched her brother. He approached the water's edge with care. Slowly extending the pole, he dropped the loop over the snake's head and jerked it back quickly. The snake writhed and rattled, but finally went limp. Tonio pulled the snake off the branch and up on the bank where Anita was waiting. She dropped the heavy rock on the snake's head and killed it.

"Good. Now I need another branch with a hook on the end to snag the basket before it floats away. Here's one." Tonio took off his boots and high socks, rolled up his pants, and said, "Get my *reata*. I'd better put the loop around my waist and have you tie the other end to Chocolate's saddle horn. Then if I fall in, you can pull me out."

"You always plan ahead, don't you?" Anita handed him the looped end of the *reata* and tied the other end to Chocolate's saddle.

"Here goes!" With the *reata* secured around his waist, Tonio stepped into the water. "Eyah! *Chihuahua*! That's cold." He snagged the tightly woven reed basket, pulled it toward himself, and laid it gently on the bank.

Anita picked up the baby. He stopped crying immediately. Then his little face puckered up as if he had tasted a sour lemon. He began to shriek again and again.

"He's hungry, poor little thing. Let's get home as fast as

we can."

"Just let me put on my socks and boots and coil up my *reata*. I hope I dry off quickly. That water was cold."

Anita took off her jacket and wrapped it around the baby. "There, there, Moisés, don't cry. We'll take you home and you'll be all right."

"Moisés? Why do you call him Moisés?" asked her brother, struggling to put his wet feet into dry socks.

"'We found him in the bulrushes, didn't we? What else should we call him? Here, you hold him while I get up on Chocolate. Lift him up to me, and I'll carry him home. You bring along that beautiful basket. We may be able to find out who his mother is. She probably made it."

Tonio and Anita set off at a fast lope along the trail to the ranch house. The baby lay quietly in her arms protected from the cool breeze by her jacket.

Doña Francisca, Tía Luisa and María Isabel were sitting in the *sala* putting the finishing touches on a new quilt when they heard excited voices outside. They heard Anita calling and Chocolate's hoofs walking up to the porch. "Mother! Tía Luisa! Come outside and see what I found."

"I wonder what it is this time," said María Isabel. "A bird with a broken wing?"

"Or a clutch of baby horned toads?" Tía Luisa shuddered. "Anita thinks they're so cute."

"It had better not be another baby fawn," said Doña Francisca in a firm voice. "Sisquoc gives me enough trouble as it is."

From the patio the excited voices of Beatriz and Tomás and other members of the family told them that whatever Anita had found, it was something quite different. Doña Francisca stuck her needle into her pin cushion and stepped briskly out to the porch. There was Anita holding a little round bundle wrapped in her leather riding jacket. Tonio, who seemed to have fallen into the river, held a large Chumash basket balanced on his saddle.

"It's a baby," announced Anita with a happy smile. "A Chumash baby. I call him Moisés because I found him in the river in the bulrushes.

Doña Francisca came over to take the baby, but Beatriz reached him first. She cuddled him in her arms. The baby sucked his left thumb and grabbed her long black braid with his tiny right hand.

"His mother must be going crazy with grief," said Doña Francisca. "José, what should we do?"

"Lorenzo, ride off to the Mission and tell the *padre* immediately," said Don José. Tomás, you ride out to see your brother's family in the Chumash *ranchería* and find out if anyone has heard of a missing baby."

"Can't we keep him?" Anita felt disappointed. Her smile faded.

"Of course," answered Doña Francisca, "but only until we find his mother and father. They must be very worried."

The baby's face puckered up again. He pulled his thumb from his mouth with a loud hungry cry. "Beatriz, take him into the kitchen and give him some warm fresh goat's milk mixed with boiled water. Mind you, the water must be boiled. Amelia," Doña Francisca said to one of the maids, "you'll find some baby clothes in that old chest in the storeroom. Bring them out along with the old cradle. As soon as he's comfortable, he'll go to sleep. He's a fine, healthy baby. How anxious his poor mother must feel."

Don José called Tonio and Anita away from the crowd of chattering maids that surrounded the baby. He brought them into his office and said, "Now tell me the whole story. Tonio, you start."

"We were riding along the river trail," Tonio began, "looking for stray cows or calves and checking the river to see if it had changed course."

"Then we heard the dogs and saw the *vaqueros* led by El Malo chasing after something or somebody about a mile away," said Anita.

"Why do you say it was El Malo? How could you recognize him a mile away?"

"He wears a silver band on his hat. It was flashing in the sunlight," answered Anita. "As soon as they saw us they turned and went back to their own land."

Don José frowned. "Think carefully. Did you see or hear anyone else? Did you see an Indian girl perhaps?"

"No," said Tonio, "we heard the baby crying. Then Anita found him in a bed of cattails."

"First, we had to kill the rattlesnake though," said Anita with a proud smile. "You should have seen how cleverly Tonio pulled it away from the baby, Father."

Tonio rolled his eyes at his sister. She had promised not to tell on him.

Don José looked at him sternly. "You had better tell me all about that, my son."

"Father, it was easy, just like catching a big lizard. That's all."

"That's all?" His father sputtered. "You both could have been bitten."

"Tonio was very careful," put in Anita, trying to help. "Besides. it wasn't very big, only about two feet long."

"Long enough to be deadly," replied Don José. "Don't you know that even a tiny rattlesnake just born can kill a small child with one bite? Don't say one word about the snake to anyone, not even your mother. Especially your mother, or she won't let you two go off riding by yourselves anymore. Tonio, you'd better run along and change into dry clothes so you don't catch cold."

Tonio left with a happy grin, glad to have gotten off easily. Don José never suspected how many rattlesnakes his son had caught, and then released, on the hilly slopes of Rancho del Mar.

"And so, Anita," said Don José, "another adventure, eh?"

"Father, you should have seen Tonio. He was so careful. He tied the *reata* around his waist, so he wouldn't be carried away by the river. He even took off his boots and socks to keep them dry."

Don José smiled. "I'm proud of you both. You and Tonio make quite a pair. Mind you, not one word about the snake to your mother."

"Father, isn't it exciting? I feel like Pharaoh's daughter in the Bible story when she found the baby in the bulrushes and took him home to raise him."

"You are my princess, Anita, but I am not the Pharaoh of Egypt." Don José's face was serious. "We can't raise the baby on Rancho del Mar. We must give him back to his parents as soon as we can find them. Lorenzo will return in a few hours. We'll see what the *padre* has to tell us."

Anita hugged her father and went off to the kitchen where she found the baby asleep in the cradle, surrounded by an adoring court of servants, just like a prince of Egypt.

Later that afternoon Lorenzo returned from Mission San Buenaventura to say that Padre Ordaz had not heard of any missing baby, nor had he baptized a baby recently. "The *padre* will send word out along the Chumash talk line to the *rancherías*. As soon as the baby's family is found, he will let us know. He asks us to bring the baby to the Mission next Sunday for baptism."

"I want to be godmother," Anita said quickly. "I found him."

"I guess that means I should be the godfather," said Don José, "so I can keep an eye on the godmother."

Lorenzo asked, "Little sister, are you sure you know enough Bible history so you can teach Moisés what he should know?"

"Yes, of course she does," answered Tía Luisa. "Probably more than you do, Lorenzo. She will be a good godmother."

The following Sunday morning Don José and his sons rode to the Mission alongside the *carreta* carrying Anita, Doña Francisca, María Isabel, Tía Luisa, and Beatriz, who was holding the baby. Although the *padre's* messengers passed the story along to the distant Chumash *rancherías,* no one came forward to claim the baby.

While the Mission bells rang in the tower, little Moisés slept soundly, wrapped in his soft, white, wool blanket. When the *padre* poured the water of baptism on the baby's head, he shrieked in dismay. Anita could not stop him from crying and handed him to Beatriz. Moisés put his left fist in his mouth. He grabbed her glossy black braid with his right hand. Then he took his fist out of his mouth and looked around with approval at everyone. "Brzhh!" he observed contentedly, put his fist in his mouth again and went back to sleep.

"I think he likes the name, 'Moisés.'" Anita felt quite grown up as she watched the *padre* take out the big Baptismal Book and write the date, the baby's name, and then her name and her father's name as godparents.

After the ceremony, the *carreta* with its passengers and mounted escort returned through the sunshine to Rancho del Mar. In the courtyard the maids had set up a table for *merienda*. Soon everyone from Don José to the youngest *vaquero* was celebrating the christening. They drank fruit juice and ate slices of watermelon. The maids served platters of *panecito*, a special bread made for the occasion.

Tomás placed Moisés' cradle in the shade of the porch where everyone could see the baby and admire him. María Isabel sat nearby playing rollicking melodies on her guitar. In the middle of the festivities there was a sudden hush. María Isabel's long fingers stilled the guitar. The *vaqueros* stopped joking and laughing.

Through the courtyard gate walked three dignified Chumash: an old village chief in ceremonial dress accompanied by his wife in her best clothes; and a young man with a sad face.

Don José stepped forward and welcomed the strangers with his courtly good manners. "Tomás, speak to them in Chumash and invite them to eat and drink with us."

"This is Chief Santiago, his wife, Catarina, and their son-in-law, Sebastián," Tomás replied.

The two older Chumash looked about sadly as they spoke to Tomás. Suddenly young Sebastián darted to the cradle on the porch. With tears in his eyes, he picked up Moisés, held him close in his arms, and carried him to the chief and his wife.

Chief Santiago, who had been educated at the Mission, said to Don José in clear Spanish. "Thank you for saving my grandson."

Don José called Anita and Tonio over to meet the chief. "My son and daughter found the baby floating in the river and brought him home."

Speaking in Chumash so that Catarina and Sebastián could understand, Tomás told about the baptism that morning. "Don José and Niña Ana are his godparents.

They named the baby Moisés."

"A good name," said Chief Santiago. "He will be a leader of his people."

The young father held Moisés high in the air. The baby laughed out loud. Then Beatriz led the chief and his wife to the shady *ramada* where they drank fruit juice and ate *panecito*.

Tonio walked over to Sebastián and showed him the intricately woven Chumash basket. Sebastián touched it with gentle fingers and spoke softly in Chumash. "This is why she was taken by El Malo. Gabriela was known for her weaving and for her beautiful baskets. They kidnapped her and the baby and forced her to weave blankets and baskets on their ranch."

Chief Santiago said in a deep voice, "Word came to us along the Chumash talk line that Gabriela had run away from the *rancho* the third day of the big rain, taking the baby with her. Sebastián went out alone to find them. He saw El Malo and his men returning from the river and hid himself in the *chaparral*. After they had gone, he followed the trail to the river where he found Gabriela's footprints going down the bank. He searched downstream until he saw a place where two riders dismounted and killed a snake. He found the prints of bare feet and the imprint of a basket in the mud. He found no trace of Gabriela. He saw where two persons had remounted their horses and ridden back toward Rancho del Mar. Sebastián came home to our *ranchería* just as a messenger arrived with news of a baby found in a basket in the river. We believe that Gabriela drowned. She would never leave the baby alone."

Anita and Tonio listened with close attention to the chief's story. Anita's eyes filled with tears. Tonio was relieved to see that his mother was busy talking to Catarina and did not hear the chief mention a snake. Beatriz was translating from Spanish to Chumash so that Catarina would understand.

Doña Francisca took Don José aside and whispered, "José, we can't let them walk back all the way to the *ranchería.*'"

"I'll give them some horses, Francisca."

"And blankets," added his wife. "They'll need blankets and food. Catarina says they have a goat, so Moisés will have milk to drink. José, I don't think there is much food in their village."

Don José looked fondly at his wife. "You have a kind heart, *querida.*" He ordered a *vaquero* to fill several saddlebags with large pieces of fresh beef. He told Tomás to bring three steady horses from the corral.

Chief Santiago accepted the gifts with great dignity. Then he said, "El Malo will take the horses away from us."

"No matter. We have many horses. I would not want you to walk all the way home."

Doña Francisca gave Catarina wool blankets and a bottle of goat's milk and boiled water for the baby. Catarina placed the beautiful basket in Doña Francisca's hands saying "Gabriela would want you to have this, señora."

Doña Francisca held the basket carefully and said, "Catarina, it will always be very precious to me."

The Chumash mounted the horses. Beatriz handed Moisés up to his grandmother. Moisés cried. He wanted to go back to Beatriz. To comfort himself, he put his left fist in his mouth, grabbed his grandmother's long braid with his right hand, and held it tight.

"Goodbye, Moisés. I'll come and see you someday," Anita promised. She felt both glad and sad as she watched Moisés ride away safe and secure in his grandmother's arms.

The Chumash family rode off to their *ranchería* taking a trail that did not go through the land managed by El Malo. Anita and Tonio walked to the kitchen with Beatriz who wore a pleased smile on her face.

"I think Moisés liked me," she said. "Did you hear how he cried for me to hold him? Don't you think he loves me a little, Niña Ana?"

"Of course he does. How could he not love you? We all love you, Beatriz."

"Sure, even that sailor. You remember Barbaroja, don't you?" teased Tonio. He snatched the last three pieces of *panecito* off a plate, dodged around Beatriz, and slipped out the door.

ON THE SESPE

The *adobe* **walls** of the ranch house glowed like gold in the rays of the setting sun. If only it were real gold, Anita thought, as she sat on the porch hemming a blouse. Her father entered the courtyard gateway weary from a long day in the saddle. The silver spurs on his boots jingled musically with each long stride. She put aside her sewing and ran to meet him. He kissed her and tugged playfully at her thick black curls. "I need to talk to Lorenzo."

"Here I am," said his eldest son. He was twenty years old, tall, lean and athletic. He looks just like Father must have looked when he was young, Anita said to herself.

"Don Mateo Quintero hasn't returned the load of hay and barley we lent him last month," said Don José. "We're running out of feed. If I order more from Santa Barbara, the ranch will be in debt. That's something I want to avoid. Tomorrow you had better go and see when he can return the hay and grain."

"Father, I'd like to visit Baby Moisés." As the baby's godmother, Anita took her responsibilities very seriously.

"I can take her to the *ranchería*," Lorenzo offered. "Tonio could come along too. He can keep her out of trouble."

Anita swallowed the hot words forming in her throat. It's hard to act grown up, she thought, when people keep treating me like a baby. She held her tongue. If she protested, they might not let her go. In the 1830's in Old California, it was not customary for a *ranchero's* daughter to make an overnight trip on horseback unless the whole family and most of the servants went along. "Please, Father, let me go with Lorenzo."

Don José smiled at his young daughter. He rarely refused her anything she wanted. "Very well. Be careful, Lorenzo. Take two muskets and a carbine. You may meet a grizzly or a cougar in Sespe Canyon."

Early the next morning Anita felt like a grownup as a *vaquero* slipped the carbine into its leather holster on Chocolate's saddle. The short barreled carbine, like the long barreled muskets, was a muzzle loader. Powder and shot had to be poured down the muzzle and then tamped down with a rod. Don José had taught her how to load and fire it.

Facing into the sun the three young riders set off up the Santa Clara River Valley toward the Quintero ranch. They arrived at sunset and were immediately asked to stay a few days. Don Mateo was famous for his hospitality. The six fun loving Quintero girls turned an ordinary dinner into a party, but the next morning shortly after dawn the young

Lorenzanas had to leave

"Goodbye, Doña Alicia. Goodbye, Don Mateo. Thank you for your hospitality," said Anita.

Mi casa es suya," replied Don Mateo.

"Goodbye, girls," Tonio gave an airy wave of his hand to the six Quintero sisters who stood by the porch railing like steps on stairs.

After raising his hat respectfully to Doña Alicia, Lorenzo led his brother and sister away from the *rancho* to a trail that followed Sespe Creek. "I came here once with Tomás," he said. "The trail over the mountains should be about four miles to the east. I think I can find it. The *ranchería* is on the other side of this range of mountains."

"Too bad the sky is covered with gray clouds," remarked Tonio. "The Chumash *vaquero* who saddled my horse told me it would rain today, very hard."

"We don't want to be caught on Sespe Creek during a heavy rain," said Lorenzo with an anxious look at the sky. "That gentle little creek can become a raging river."

"If it starts raining too hard, we'll just turn back," said Anita. "We can visit the *ranchería* another time. We can always go the other way, around the mountains and through the Ventura River Valley."

"This is a good trail. The ancient Chumash used it." Lorenzo looked at the sky again and pressed on through the canyon. The horses picked their way between the boulders and down the steep places under the trees.

"Lorenzo, look." Tonio pointed to bear droppings along the edge of the creek. "Right near that growth of berry bushes. Tomás says those berries have a thick, sweet skin that bears love to eat."

"That's just great," answered Lorenzo. "All we need is a couple of grizzly bears and a heavy rain." He changed the subject. "The Quinteros have lost their ranch to Señor Valencia. Don Mateo told me so this morning. He was ashamed to say he couldn't return the feed he borrowed from us. We really need the grain. Father doesn't like to buy it on credit. Maybe he'll have to."

I hope we never lose our ranch, Anita said to herself; I'd just die if we had to leave it and go somewhere else.

"How did it happen that Don Mateo is losing his ranch?" Tonio wanted to know.

"He gave too many lavish fiestas and gambled too often at cards and on horse races," answered his brother. "Señor Valencia lent him money. When his grassland burnt up in that fire last summer and the cattle died, Don Mateo couldn't pay his debts. Now Señor Valencia is taking over the ranch."

Tonio opened his water flask and took a drink. "Tomás believes that fire was set. Our grass would have burnt up too, but we were lucky. Just as the flames reached our land, a sea wind came up and blew the fire back on itself."

"Father told me that Don Mateo doesn't know anything about running a ranch," said Lorenzo. He studied the clouds overhead.

"Mother says the ranch really belongs to Doña Alicia whose father was very rich. He owned a large *hacienda* in Mexico," put in Anita. "Mother says that Doña Alicia fell in love with Don Mateo because he is so handsome, has nice manners, and sings and plays the guitar so well."

"Tía Luisa says that he married her for her money," added Tonio.

Anita looked at Tonio. "Tía Luisa says there should be a law that lets a wife take care of her *rancho* and manage her own money after she marries."

"Hah!" jeered Tonio. "Who ever heard of a woman

running a *rancho?*"

"How would she deal with the *vaqueros?* asked Lorenzo. "I can't see a head *vaquero* like Tomás being ordered around by a woman."

"He always does everything Beatriz asks him to do," said his sister. "Now if I were running a *rancho,* I would have somebody like you give the orders to the *vaqueros.* Father says the ranching business is a matter of not spending more than your income."

"That must be why he counts every cow hide, every sheepskin and every bag of tallow," said Tonio.

"Too bad Doña Alicia didn't have a good manager." Lorenzo looked at the darkening sky. "Now they are all going back to Mexico City. Doña Alicia has a rich uncle there with no family and a big house. His friends are all rich too."

"That will be good because they have to find husbands for their six girls." I hope I never have to leave Rancho del Mar, Anita thought. She frowned at the idea. We'd have to go to Mexico City. Girls don't go out of the house without chaperones there. I couldn't go riding when I wanted to. There would be no blue ocean, no whales spouting, no golden poppies on the hills, no sunsets that take your breath away. I wouldn't like it there at all. We would have to depend on our relatives, just like the Quinteros. That would be awful.

The sky grew darker and a slight drizzle began to fall. "We'd better stop and put on our *ponchos,*" said Lorenzo. "Your *vaquero* friend certainly knew what the weather would be like around here, Tonio."

They reined in the horses and took out the *ponchos.* Anita took the smallest one. She put her head through the hole in the center. The wool blanket fell around her shoulders and down to her ankles. When she remounted Chocolate, the edges of the *poncho* fell down around the saddle.

"Are you expecting heavy rain, Lorenzo?" asked Tonio.

"I'm going to play it safe and look for the cave Tomás and I stayed in. I know it's not far from here."

Horses and riders picked their way along the uneven trail that wandered through the rugged beauty of the canyon. Sandstone cliffs loomed up on either side and the smell of wet pine needles filled the air. Anita noticed that the water in Sespe Creek was much higher than it had been an hour ago. She saw Lorenzo look at the rising water and spur his horse forward.

Tonio's keen eyes glanced up the canyon. He pointed to a sandstone ledge jutting out of the cliff. "Is that the cave?"

"I see it. That's the one. Let's get over there right now."

Large drops of rain were falling. By the time they reached the cave, water was dripping off their wide-brimmed hats and running down over their backs, but the thick woolen *ponchos* kept them dry and warm.

"Tie up the horses to those heavy rocks under the overhang. I'm going to find some wood that is still dry enough to burn," said Lorenzo. "Stack the muskets in a dry place where we can reach them quickly if we need them."

They dismounted. Anita and Tonio led the horses under the overhang out of the rain and tied them fast to the heavy rocks on the ledge. They stacked the muskets and the powder horns in the dry cave entrance.

"Wait here," said Tonio to Anita. "I want to check the cave first and make sure we will not be sharing it with a sleeping bear, or a wildcat, or even bats," he added with a grin. After loading his musket he held it in a ready position and disappeared into the shadows of the cave.

"Bats?" Anita called after him. "Beatriz says they get in your hair. I won't go in that cave if there are bats on the ceiling."

Tonio returned from his search. "Too bad. No bears, no wildcats, no bats. Not even a snake." He unloaded the musket and set it upright alongside the others.

"Thanks, I think," replied his sister. She took the saddle-bags and brought them inside the cave.

Tonio unsaddled the horses and carried the saddles inside out of the rain. "These will be our pillows tonight."

Lorenzo made four trips through the rain for firewood. He lit a small fire at the opposite end of the ledge from the horses. He chose a spot where the smoke would blow away from the cave entrance. While he prepared the fire, Anita and Tonio took out a mixture of grain and hay from their supplies and fed the horses.

"That's a good fire," Lorenzo said with satisfaction as the wood crackled and burned. "It will keep away wild animals. We may have to spend two days here." He held his cold hands out to the fire.

"Well, we certainly won't be short of water," his sister answered.

The rain was pouring down in sheets. The mild Sespe Creek had become a roaring river. Upstream heavy boulders crashed and thundered to the canyon floor as the heavy rain coursed down the canyon walls. They sat and watched the downpour from a dry place under the overhang.

Tonio disappeared in the shadows behind them and then rejoined his brother and sister. "Come and see the strange pictures on the wall back there."

Lorenzo and Anita followed him to the back of the cave. It smelled musty, like an animal's den. In the fading light, they could see the strange red and black markings painted on the rock wall. There were small circles and little stick figures about three hands high, "Tomás told me that these were made by the Chumash holy men a long time ago." said Lorenzo. "This cave was a holy place where they would come to pray and draw these figures."

"I'm glad to know that," said Anita. "I won't be afraid to go to sleep in a holy place. Are you sure there are no bats, Tonio?"

"No bats," he answered and turned toward the entrance. "Let's eat while it's still light. I'm hungry again."

With their backs against the rock wall, they warmed their feet by the fire and ate hard boiled eggs, dried apricots, and *machacas* made of beans, shredded beef and chile pepper wrapped in flour *tortillas*. They drank the cold rain water dripping down from the rocks above.

"Father was right, Anita." Lorenzo smiled as he peeled an egg. "Adventure follows you wherever you go, like a bear follows a bee to a honey tree."

"I can't help it if things happen." His sister's voice sounded tired. They tease me about bringing home a little fawn or a couple of horned toads, she thought, but not about finding *diseños* or Chumash babies.

"Nobody is complaining." Tonio assured her. "Why, I just love to eat cold beans instead of hot barbecued beef and drink cold water instead of hot chocolate."

"All right, now. Let's have no more of that kind of talk," said Lorenzo. "The Chumash would be very happy to eat your cold beans tonight, little brother."

"Beatriz told me that food is scarce on the *rancherías*," Anita worried. "Most of the Chumash have forgotten how to hunt wild game. When the Mexican government sent them away from the missions, they had forgotten how to make bows and arrows the way their grandfathers did.

They raise a little corn, gather acorns and trap rabbits, but it's not enough. I hope Moisés is all right."

"We'll see how he is tomorrow." Lorenzo yawned. Then he sat up, tense and alert. "Listen, do you hear anything?"

"Something's out there, all right," whispered Tonio. "The horses are restless."

"Load the guns quickly."

They loaded the muskets and the carbine carefully, and waited. Then a blood-curdling scream like a woman in agony came from the rocks overhead. They leaped to their horses. Anita grabbed Chocolate's reins before he could tear himself loose. Lorenzo and Tonio kept tight hold of their terrified animals and quieted them with soft crooning sounds and gentle petting.

"What was that?" gulped Anita.

"Mountain lion," answered Lorenzo in a tense voice. "Tie down these reins for me, Tonio, while I keep my musket ready."

"I've never heard one so close," said Tonio. "He must want to get into his cave out of the rain."

"Poor Chocolate, don't worry. It will be all right. We're here." Anita tied his reins securely around a big rock.

Lorenzo balanced his musket across his chest. "Mountain lions hate fire. That big cat won't try to come in here while it's burning."

Anita picked up a piece of wood and put it on the fire. Suddenly the cougar appeared at the end of the ledge. His topaz eyes glared fiercely at her across the flames. White fangs gleamed in the firelight. Without stopping to think, Anita grabbed a burning piece of wood, and hurled it like a javelin at the open jaws of the mountain lion. He turned away with a snarl, and leaped off the ledge into the darkness.

"I couldn't shoot." Lorenzo was breathing hard. His face was a sickly white. "You were between me and the lion."

Wide eyed and open mouthed, Tonio gripped the reins. The horses' hoofs kicked and clattered on the rocky ledge. "*Chihuahua!* That was a close one."

Lorenzo held his musket ready. "He may come back."

Anita and Tonio held the reins tightly and waited. There was no sound except the heavy downpour of rain. Anita made up her mind to show her brothers that she was not afraid. She held Chocolate's bridle and comforted him with soft words, but her blood ran cold when the cougar screamed again. In the firelight they glimpsed the big yellow cat as he leaped from the rocks overhead and ran down the slope.

"He's gone," said Lorenzo. "Let's hobble the horses and make sure they can't run away. We might have thunder and lightning tonight."

While Lorenzo tended to the fire, Anita and Tonio secured the horses. They carried the wet *ponchos* inside the cave. Wringing out as much water as possible, they spread them out on the floor. "They're too wet to use as blankets," said Tonio. "Tonight we'll have to sleep without covers on the bare ground."

Before Anita lay her head on the saddle, she took out a large handkerchief. The thought of bats made her flesh creep. Animals that look like big-eared mice shouldn't be able to fly. You can't see them. You can't hear them. She shuddered and tied the handkerchief around her head. She was more afraid of bats than she was of the cougar.

Lorenzo laughed when he saw her wearing the kerchief. "Surely you don't believe that old story. Bats eat insects. They are not interested in your hair or mine either." He tossed more wood on the fire.

"Well, I'm going to wear my kerchief anyway," Anita said stubbornly and pillowed her head on the leather saddle.

The downpour continued. The sound of falling rain lulled them into a deep sleep. Lorenzo woke first when a ray of sunlight entered the cave and fell on his upturned face.

"No more rain!" He stretched his arms and yawned. Then he pulled on his boots after shaking each one carefully to dislodge any centipedes. "Look at that blue sky. You two get our breakfast out of the saddlebags. I'll walk up the trail to check for mountain lion tracks." He took his musket and stepped down off the ledge.

"Breakfast, hmph," Tonio grumbled as he started up the fire from the glowing embers. The mountain air was cold. "We'll eat the same things we ate last night."

"Oh, stop complaining, Tonio," snapped Anita. She felt stiff and sore. "Make the best of a bad situation. That's what Mother always says."

Lorenzo came back with a glum face. "The good news is no cougar tracks. As for the bad news, a mud slide has completely blocked off the old trail. We'll have to turn back. You won't see Moisés for a while yet, Little Sister. We had better eat breakfast, then water and feed the horses and start for home."

Anita thought, I wish he wouldn't keep calling me "Little Sister." She felt less grumpy after eating some breakfast. "I'm going to wash my face and give Chocolate a drink." Taking careful steps she led Chocolate back down the muddy trail under the dripping sycamores until she found a flat place where they could reach the water. As she splashed her face in the cold water, she saw something

57

bright and glittering in the sand. She picked it up. It was heavier than it looked. A gold nugget! She shrieked. "Gold! Tonio, Lorenzo, come quickly."

They left the cave and hurried to the creek. Tonio looked at the nugget. "Is that really gold?"

"It looks like it and it's certainly heavy enough." Lorenzo weighed the nugget in his hand. "The ship's agent in Santa Barbara will be able to tell us how much it is worth."

"I see another one." Tonio pushed up his sleeve and plunged his arm in the water.

"And another one, but smaller." Anita's eyes gleamed with excitement.

"I'm going to look, too," Lorenzo shouted like a small boy as he removed his boots.

Struck with gold fever they sifted through the sand up and down the creek bed until the sun was high and their hands and feet numb with cold. Finally Tonio sighed with regret. "I don't see any more gold. How much do we have?"

Lorenzo looked at the mound of heavy nuggets and thin flakes laid out on Anita's handkerchief. "We have enough to make Rancho del Mar safe from creditors. Father will be very happy, Anita. Now he won't need to borrow any money."

"Another great adventure." Tonio grinned. "Little Sister, I'd be glad to come along with you, anywhere, anytime, rain or shine, cougars or no cougars."

"I don't plan these things. They just happen — and stop calling me 'Little Sister.' "

"Be still, both of you. We must be very cautious," Lorenzo looked sternly at his brother and sister. "Not a word to anyone until we get home. This land is held by the governor for lease, but no one wants it because it's all rocky canyons and not fit for grazing cattle. The gold belongs to us. We found it. If Señor Valencia heard about this, he would claim the gold belonged to him. His *rancho* boundary is nearby."

"Can't we go home another way?" asked Anita.

"How about heading for that empty old *adobe* on the east end of our *rancho?* The one the *vaqueros* use at roundup time," suggested Tonio.

"I had forgotten about that place." Lorenzo looked at the sun. "It's almost noon. We can reach there before dark tonight and be home tomorrow morning. The Sespe is very beautiful, but I don't trust that creek. We could have another rainstorm that would wash out this trail. Let's feed the horses and be on our way."

The sun was setting as they rode up to the old *adobe.* They hobbled the horses and let them graze before turning them into the corral for the night. The one-room *adobe* was dry inside and warmer than the cave.

Lorenzo found some dry wood piled in the corner. "Thank heaven the roof is still tight."

Soon they were huddled outside close to a warm fire eating another cold meal. Gazing into the flickering flames, Anita remembered the excitement of finding the *diseño.* She recalled with a shiver the terror of the robbery. Like a bad dream, a thought throbbed at the back of her mind. Was someone trying to ruin the family and take their ranch? Without land to raise cattle, what would they do?

"Lorenzo, just suppose we did lose the ranch in spite of everything. What would you do?"

Lorenzo stared into the fire. "Father is starting to teach me the hide business. I don't know much of anything except ranching. I really don't know what I'd do."

"Hah! Marry some rich girl, that's what you'd have to do. That's what Don Mateo Quintero did."

"Well, Tonio, what would you do?" his brother wanted to know.

For once Tonio's face became serious. "I'd probably be a *vaquero* on somebody else's ranch. I think Enrique and Fernando would have to do the same."

"We're not going to lose the ranch," Lorenzo stated in a firm voice. "We found enough gold today to keep us out of debt. Stop worrying. Let's try to get some sleep."

While her brothers settled the horses for the night, Anita picked hot embers out of the fire with two sticks. She dropped the embers in the hollowed out section of a cottonwood tree bole that the *vaqueros* used as a brazier.

Lorenzo carried the heavy wooden piece inside and set it in a corner of the room. "The embers will give off enough heat to keep us warm and comfortable through the night," he said. "The cottonwood will char, but not burn."

The *ponchos* were still damp. Again they lay down on a bare floor without covers. Tired and weary, stiff and sore, they fell asleep almost immediately.

Rising at daybreak, they ate the last of the apricots and *machacas* and drank from the small spring near the house. They fed, watered and saddled the horses. Anita tied the heavy bag of gold tightly to the cantle of Lorenzo's saddle. The empty saddlebags she divided between Tonio's saddle and her own.

"Are we ready to go?" Tonio was impatient.

"Let me check to see that the fire is completely out," said Lorenzo. "We don't want to set fire to the *adobe*."

The sun felt warm on their backs as they rode west along the river trail to the ranch house. The wet ground steamed in the early morning sunshine. There were a few dark clouds to the east, but overhead the sky was a clear deep blue. Although the Santa Clara River was running at flood level, it had stayed within its banks.

Tonio looked ahead and pointed. "Condors." Five huge birds, cousins to the vultures, circled lazily over a large grayish-white form near the sandy riverbank, "It's that wild gray stallion that grazes here. Where are all his mares and colts?"

They wheeled their horses and headed toward the grayish-white shape. "He's been shot!" Anita's dark eyes flashed. "Who would do such a thing?"

"If they wanted to steal the mares and foals, thieves would shoot the stallion first and then use their own stallion to lead the mares away." Lorenzo's face was grim. "Cold-blooded killers to destroy a beautiful horse like that."

"Who did it?" Tonio asked. "Those horse thieves from New Mexico who were operating near Mission San Fernando?"

"Whoever did it has twenty top quality mares and colts that used to belong to us," Lorenzo growled. He smacked his right fist into his left palm in helpless anger.

"Father will be furious." Anita sighed. "At least we have some good news to cancel out the bad. Let's go home. This place makes me feel so sad I want to cry." Another attack on our *rancho,* she thought. Who is doing this?

María Isabel met the three tired riders as they entered the courtyard about noon. "Father is in his office. I'll ask Beatriz to heat up some soup. You all look so cold and hungry."

"Big Sister, you're a sweetheart," said a grateful Tonio.

Lorenzo, Anita and Tonio entered Don José's office and stood before him with wide smiles. Don José looked at his three trail-weary children. "Well, you're back a day early.

Did you see Baby Moisés? Do you have a promise from Don Mateo to return the load of grain and hay?"

"Something better." Anita's wide smile brought the dimples to her cheeks. "Show him, Lorenzo."

Lorenzo lifted the small *alforja*, turned it upside down and let the heavy pieces of gold drop on his father's desk. For a moment Don José was stunned. "Gold! Enough to run Rancho del Mar free of debt for more than a year. Where did you find it?"

"I washed my face in Sespe Creek and there it was." Anita tried hard to speak in a grown-up manner. "Lorenzo, Tonio and I picked the gold out of the creek yesterday morning."

"This is magnificent." Don José touched the pile gently with his finger. Then, taking a leather pouch from his desk, he carefully dropped the gold inside. "Don't say anything to anyone yet. I want to tell the family myself. I'll put this away while you have some hot soup."

Tonio hurried away. Lorenzo and Anita lingered by the desk. "There's some bad news, too."

Don José glanced up from the leather bag held tightly in his fingers. His face clouded. He looked directly at his eldest son and braced himself. "What is it this time?"

"First, Don Mateo can't return the loan of hay and grain. He's losing the ranch to Señor Valencia. Second, horse thieves stole twenty wild mares and colts from the gray stallion's band. They shot the stallion."

Don José winced. He hit his clenched fist hard on the desk top. "That splendid horse. His band was the next one I planned to part out. There have been too many suspicious incidents lately. Someone seems to be trying to do us harm." He stood up, put his arm around Anita's waist and clapped Lorenzo on the shoulder. "We'll put that matter aside for now. You go on to the *sala* while I put this gold in a safe place."

Doña Francisca, Tía Luisa and María Isabel were waiting in the *sala* with steaming bowls of hot soup and fresh *tortillas*. Tonio had already started on his bowl. The twins, Enrique and Fernando, entered together and sat down nearby. "Did the Quinteros sell that black saddle horse?" Enrique wanted to know.

Anita, Lorenzo and Tonio were peppered with more questions. "Tell us more about the Quinteros. How is Doña Alicia?" "Are they really going back to Mexico?" "Did you see Baby Moisés and his family?" "Why did you come back early?" Little by little the story came out between mouthfuls of food.

"I know something else happened that you are not telling us about," said Doña Francisca. "Anita, you are so full of a secret that your skin is cracking, as my father used to say."

Anita smiled knowingly at Lorenzo and Tonio. They chuckled. "It's a surprise. We're not supposed to tell yet."

At that moment Don José came in with a beaming face and kissed Doña Francisca. "They had a very successful trip. They found and brought back enough gold to keep the ranch debt free for more than a year."

The twins cheered and slapped each other on the back. Doña Francisca hugged Anita. María Isabel clapped her hands. "Let's give a fiesta," cried Tía Luisa.

"With a big barbecue." Tonio was thinking of food again.

Doña Francisca began planning right away. "We haven't given a party in such a long time. I'll make a list of what we need."

Don José's face became serious. "We must keep the

gold a secret for a while yet. Lorenzo, I'll need you and Enrique and Fernando to go with me tomorrow when I take the gold to Santa Barbara. I want to put it in the de la Guerra strong room. I don't want to ride alone and meet someone like Don Ramón Gutiérrez where the surf covers the road at high tide."

"Don Ramón Gutiérrez de Navarre, don't forget," added Lorenzo.

"I won't forget him." Don José's smile was grim. "I think of him every time I put on those silver spurs."

4

ANITA GOES TO SEA

I'm off for Santa Barbara tomorrow," Don José announced at dinner. "I'll take Lorenzo along to teach him how to trade with foreign ship captains, and Enrique and Fernando should become acquainted with Don José de la Guerra. He is a very important man in Santa Barbara."

"Please, Father, take me too," Anita begged. "I promise to keep out of trouble. I won't lag behind. I'll ride Azúcar. She can travel for hours and never get tired."

"No," said Don José. "This is a business trip, not a fiesta. We'll be staying at the de la Guerra home. After I put the gold in the strong room, I have important ranch business to discuss with him."

Anita pestered and pestered her father until he finally relented and said she could come along. "No more adventures," he warned her.

"Remember your manners," said Doña Francisca to her sons. "Don't forget to curtsy when you meet an older person, Anita. Eat slowly. Listen to what the grown-ups are saying, but don't interrupt with questions."

With a mischievous smile at María Isabel, who had wanted to go along, Anita mounted Azúcar and turned north on Camino Real with her father and brothers. According to California custom the Lorenzanas galloped for some distance, rested their horses by walking them, and galloped again. Azúcar seemed to enjoy the trip as much as her rider.

They arrived about noon at the large and comfortable de la Guerra *adobe* in plenty of time for dinner at two o'clock. Anita quickly made friends with the de la Guerra children. There were five boys and four girls. Two of the girls were close to her in age. It's fun to talk to someone else who's twelve years old, she thought. They understand me. I wish we lived closer.

Like a proper young lady, the youngest Lorenzana curtsied to Don José and Doña Antonia de la Guerra and the other guests including a large number of Americans. She listened attentively to the conversations at the dinner table.

The Californians don't like Governor Chico, she thought. On the other hand, he doesn't like Californians. He placed Señor Carrillo under house arrest. They say the governor imposes restrictions in accordance with Mexican law. He pays no attention to California ways of doing things. The Americans listen and say nothing at all when his name is mentioned. I wonder what they think about him.

Their friend, Captain Caleb Biddle, the Yankee sea captain from Boston, paid a courtesy call on the de la

Guerras in the late afternoon. He strode into the patio where the guests had gathered and paid his respects to his host. Catching sight of Anita and her father, he walked through the chattering crowd to greet them.

"He's a blue water sailor," whispered Don José to Anita. "See how he puts his feet down firmly with each step as if he were on a rolling deck."

"This is an unexpected pleasure," said Captain Biddle.

"Glad to see you again," replied Don José.

The captain must have shaved off his beard yesterday, Anita thought. His forehead, cheeks and nose were tanned but the skin along his jaw-line was sunburned. The sun had bleached his sandy hair almost white and his eyes were blue as summer seas. Although not as tall as Don José, the captain's compact body was muscular and well knit. He spoke a correct rather quaint kind of Castilian Spanish with many Argentine and Chilean words.

"My daughter, Martha, is the same age as you are." The lines at the corners of his eyes crinkled as he smiled at Anita. "Don José, I would like you and your children to come aboard for Sunday dinner on my brig, the *Pride of Nantucket*. We'll be sailing south to San Diego on Monday."

"Anita and I would enjoy that very much, Captain, but my sons promised to visit friends on a ranch near Santa Barbara and will not be able to come."

On Sunday a manservant of the de la Guerras drove Anita and Don José to the harbor where the *Pride of Nantucket* was anchored. As their carriage passed the Customs Office, closed on Sunday of course, Anita thought how much the harbor had changed since the previous year. There were so many people, strange looking people from the half dozen ships of all sizes and shapes anchored off shore. Blond Americans from Boston mingled with the crowd of tall, brown Pacific Islanders with tattooed faces, black men from Cuba, and Chinese from Canton. She even saw two American ladies, who were sea captains' wives, wearing odd looking hats called "bonnets."

Small boats, rowed by sturdy seamen, were coming and going, picking up supplies or carrying passengers from the ships to the shore. As they walked across the broad beach toward the longboat, Don José carefully noted the number of hides and leather bags of tallow stacked on the sand ready to be loaded aboard the Yankee and British trading ships.

Two strong sailors with tattooed arms rowed Anita and her father out to the ship. She tried not to stare as their rippling muscles pulled on the oars, making tattooed ships move up and down on tattooed seas. One sailor gently lifted Anita out of the long boat to the ship's ladder and she climbed aboard.

The ship was a strange kind of place, very different from land. How clean and neat everything is, she thought. Anita looked at the wooden deck, so smooth and white under her feet, the ropes coiled neatly in place, and the brass fittings shining in the sunlight. Overhead the two masts towered above her. The spars or cross pieces held the furled sails. She sniffed the faint scent of tar and newly cut lumber.

Captain Biddle met them at the top of the ladder. "*Buenos días*. Welcome aboard." He showed the way into his cabin where a long table of highly polished dark wood was set for three.

The cook served them a New England dinner of boiled California beef, potatoes and onions. Anita didn't really care for the boiled dinner, but ate some anyway to be polite.

For dessert they had Indian pudding, "a Boston favorite," the captain said. Then the cook brought in a large bowl filled with fresh fruit from the Mission and set it on the table. He poured tea into pretty blue and white cups. Anita remembered that Doña Antonia served chocolate in the same kind of cups

"These cups and saucers are from Canton, China," said Captain Biddle, "and so is the tea." Anita had never tasted tea before. She liked it very much. Maybe Father will buy some to bring home, she thought.

After dinner Captain Biddle and Don José began to talk of business matters. Excusing herself, Anita went outside, stood by the railing, and looked across the harbor to Santa Barbara. In the late afternoon sunlight she could see the treeless mountains overlooking the red roofed houses below. High up on the hillside the white mission tower stood out clearly. Its ringing bells echoed from the hills. She noticed that the sky had turned a strange dark color and a sudden sea wind was blowing her hair about. The ship began moving up and down in the waves like a galloping horse. Frightened out of her wits, Anita gripped the rail tightly.

A sailor lying nearby on the deck jumped to his feet and ran to the door of the captain's cabin. "Captain Biddle, sir, you had best come look at the weather. The wind has changed."

Captain Biddle had already sensed a change in his ship. He came out on deck and looked at the dark clouds, wavy and gray underneath. The brig rolled and bucked in waves four or five feet high. "Southeaster blowing, Mr. Starbuck," he called to the mate. "Make ready to get under way."

"All hands on deck." Mr. Starbuck's roar carried to

every corner of the ship. The bos'n's pipe whistled shrilly. Sailors, who had been sleeping in the sun on deck, jumped to their stations. Others hurried up from below. "Raise the longboat." Two sailors pulled on the ropes. The longboat was raised to the deck and firmly secured. "Set the flying jib and jibsail and hoist the spanker aft. Hands forward to raise the anchor."

The ship rolled and bounced up and down like a wild thing struggling to be free. Anita's white-knuckled fingers gripped the railing. Her feet slipped out from under her, but she held on. Her heart thudded in her chest. A big lump rose in her throat. *"Ave María Puríssima!"* Anita prayed. The gently rolling sea of early afternoon had turned into an angry monster that terrified her.

A short distance away her father called from the doorway of the captain's cabin. "Come inside, out of the way. We can stand in the doorway and watch."

For a moment she couldn't move. Her feet seemed frozen to the deck. Helpless, she looked at her father. He knew that she was paralyzed with fear and held out his arms to her. She jerked herself free from the railing and stumbled across the deck. Hiding her face in her father's coat, she moaned, "I want to go home to Rancho del Mar."

Don José held her tightly. "Don't be afraid. It's all right. Captain Biddle knows what to do. In a few minutes the ship will stop bucking."

Although her father's soothing voice calmed Anita, she was still afraid, but it was much easier to face the unknown with her father's arms around her. She held on to him tightly and watched the sailors.

Each member of the crew stood at his station. Close by the cabin doorway, two sailors pulled on the halyards to hoist the spanker. At the same time other seamen hoisted the flying jib and jibsail. When the halyards were made fast, the men ran forward to help the others raise the anchor. Slowly chanting, "Yo, heave, ho," they pushed on the spokes of the big wheel. The heavy anchor hawser rose dripping from the sea and wound around the capstan.

"Helmsman," ordered the captain, "set course west by southwest."

As the helmsman turned her on course, the *Pride of Nantucket* spread out her wings like a giant bird. Guided by the southeast winds and the rudder, she turned to the west. Other ships were spreading their sails to leave the harbor and head out to sea.

"Don José," said Captain Biddle, "we must move out of the harbor before the southeaster makes us run aground at Santa Barbara Point. We will be sailing to San Diego a day early. I am sorry, but it is not possible to put you ashore. We'll bring you back to Santa Barbara next week."

From a large, floating box of wood, the ship seemed to change and take on a life of her own. As the white canvas sails snapped and the wind blew through the rigging, the *Pride of Nantucket* moved through the choppy water. It's like riding Chocolate through fields of high grass, thought Anita. How I wish I were home with him now.

Don José's tanned face suddenly became quite pale. He looked sheepish as he said, "I forgot to tell you. I always get seasick the first day out on the water." He walked to the other side of the ship and bent over the rail, shoulders heaving.

Anita was so concerned about her father that she forgot to be afraid. "Come in and lie down on the bunk, Father," said Anita. "I'll get you some hot tea and you'll feel better in a little while." Don José collapsed on the bunk.

The ship sailed steadily westward out of Santa Barbara

harbor. The sun was setting and darkness was coming on. Captain Biddle set his course far to the west because he did not want the ship to crash on the rocks, or run aground in the darkness.

Entering the cabin, Captain Biddle spread his sea charts out on the table. He showed Anita the course the ship would take out of the channel. "It will be dark when we sail between the end of Santa Cruz Island and the coast," he said. "We have to keep to the middle of the channel and watch out for other ships. We must take care not to run aground."

Darkness fell and the *Pride of Nantucket* sailed on a steady course to the west. Don José stayed in his bunk, while Anita and Captain Biddle ate supper together by candlelight. The cook served Boston baked beans and brown bread. Anita thought the beans could have used a few chile peppers for flavor, but she liked the brown bread and drank two cups of the fragrant tea.

After supper Captain Biddle said, "You sleep in the other bunk, Anita. I'll go down to the first mate's cabin."

Anita climbed into the bunk, pulled the warm blanket up to her chin and listened as the ship's bell rang the half hour. She closed her eyes for an instant and fell fast asleep. In the middle of the night she woke up. The movement of the ship had changed. The warm south wind was no longer blowing and the ship no longer bucked like an unbroken horse. The sea had flattened out. She heard the captain tell the helmsman, "Steer course east by southeast." She turned her head on the pillow and slept.

At daybreak she stepped out on deck with Don José to see the headlands of Santa Cruz Island on the right. The wind blew steadily from the northwest. Anita heard Mr. Starbuck bellow an order. "Set fore and main topsails, t'gallants and royals." Sailors leaped into the rigging, climbed up the masts like acrobats and ran out along the spars. On the deck below, other sailors hauled on the halyards. As the sails filled with wind, the *Pride of Nantucket* cut through the waves. She thought, the helmsman at the wheel holds the ship on course the way I use the bridle to guide Chocolate.

Captain Biddle joined Anita and her father as they stood by the rail, "We'll be in San Diego in three days."

"We are so close to San Buenaventura," said Don José, "Couldn't you bring the ship closer to shore and let us land on the beach?"

"I am sorry, Don José," said the captain. "If I set you ashore, I would lose a whole day with the wind blowing the way it is now. I have to give account to the owners for each day spent at sea because each day at sea costs them money. I must follow orders." He turned to Anita and said, "We'll be passing San Buenaventura Mission very soon. See how the mountains come down close to the shore?"

"Yes," she answered, "That's where the road to Santa Barbara is squeezed between the mountains and the sea. We often must wait there at high tide because the water covers the road."

"Look," Don José pointed to the shoreline. "The Santa Clara Valley opens up into a wide, flat plain. Rancho del Mar is in a fine location, indeed. There's a good climate, a gentle slope to the land and a plentiful supply of water in the river. I have never seen it from the sea before." Then he and Captain Biddle walked away aft talking about the hide trade.

Anita stood alone by herself on deck and watched as the ship sailed past Santa Cruz Island. Up ahead familiar Anacapa Island was in sight. She looked toward the shore and saw the white bell tower of Mission San Buenaventura, the mission by the sea. The ship sailed on eastward through the channel. Soon Anita saw a column of smoke rising from Rancho del Mar. She knew that her mother, her aunt and her sister were in the big room downstairs. Doña Francisca would be hemming a shirt for Lorenzo, Tía Luisa embroidering a blouse, and María Isabel strumming her guitar. Soon the three would be singing together. Outside Beatriz was no doubt preparing to bake bread in the big round oven. Anita could almost smell it.

A lump rose in her throat and she felt very homesick. Her eyes filled with tears. As she wiped them away, a harsh but friendly voice said, "What's the matter, little one?"

She turned to see a small, weatherbeaten man with gray hair and bright blue eyes sitting against the cabin wall out of the wind. He was surrounded by yards of white canvas. His brown hand moved up and down as he punched thread through the canvas mending the rips in a sail.

"That's my home," she said. "That's Rancho del Mar. See the smoke rising from the bake oven?" She added politely, "My name is Anita."

The sailmaker spoke to her in words that were not really Spanish although they sounded like Spanish. He had four teeth missing in front which made him a little hard to understand at first.

"My name is Paolo," he said. "I am Portuguese, from the Azores." He told her that when he was twelve, he sailed on a fishing boat to the Grand Banks. His boat was wrecked in a storm, and he was saved by Yankee fishermen from Gloucester. "They took me home with them and then I went to Boston."

"Boston? That's where Captain Biddle comes from."

"Yes, it's a big city with many ships. I wanted to see

more of the world so I signed on board a whaler. We sailed down the coast of South America and around Cape Horn. I thought we would be sunk by the icebergs and bad storms, but our captain brought us through. We sailed all over the Pacific Ocean hunting whales for their oil. People need the oil to light the lamps in their houses. Our ship visited Honolulu in the Sandwich Islands, Manila in the Philippines and Hong Kong and Canton in China. Six years went by before we returned to Boston."

"I sailed again and again on the whalers, but one day I got sick aboard a New Bedford whaler. I had to leave the ship and go ashore. When I got well, I knew I wasn't strong enough to throw the harpoon any more, so I signed on with Captain Biddle as sailmaker."

"Do you ever feel afraid in the storms?"

"Yes, sometimes, but I always trust the captain to bring us through."

"Don't you ever go back home?" asked Anita.

"This ship is my home. I don't go ashore much. I'm half way around the world from the Azores. I'll probably never go back." Then his weatherbeaten face creased into a smile as he looked at Anita. "Wait here, little one. I have something you'll like." He went down below to his sea chest and came up with a small bundle carefully wrapped in a square of blue Chinese silk.

"I carved these years ago for my little sister," he said. "She's grown up now, and I never went back home." He handed the bundle to Anita. She opened it carefully and found five pieces of cream-colored ivory, a doll's head, two little hands and two little feet.

"I'll show you how to make a doll," said Paolo.

"What a pretty face she has. "I can make her a dress from the blue silk." Anita smiled up at him, glad for something

75

to do.

Paolo showed Anita how to make the doll from scraps of light canvas. She stuffed the body, arms and legs with hemp fiber from old pieces of rope. Then she sewed on the head, hands and feet. "When I finish the dress the canvas body won't show, only her pretty hands and feet."

That evening Captain Biddle took out from his sea chest a small globe of the world. He set it on the table and pointed to California on the Pacific Ocean. He took Anita's finger in his hand and traced the course he would be taking to bring the *Pride of Nantucket* home to Boston. He drew her finger down the coast of South America and turned the globe so that she could see Cape Horn.

"Is that the bottom of the world?" she asked.

"It's like no other place on earth. It's a world of fog, huge icebergs, and violent storms." Captain Biddle took her finger and moved it up the other side of South America, across the line of the equator, and up north past Cuba and the southern United States to the hook of Cape Cod, and across the bay to Boston.

"The voyage home will take about five months. I'll be glad to see my family again."

Anita asked more questions. "Where are the Azores?" The captain pointed to them. They were way across the Atlantic to the east, near Africa. "Where are Manila, Hong Kong and Canton?" She held the globe in her hands a long time studying it. What a big world it is, she thought. Rancho del Mar is just a tiny speck on the face of the earth.

On their last evening at sea, Anita went out on deck after dinner. She stood up in the bow, the forward part of the ship, and watched a school of playful dolphins chase each other back and forth across the bow. They could swim faster than the ship was sailing. Sometimes they would dive down and come up on the other side of the ship. She saw them smiling as they raced along. "Come, Anita. Come play tag with us," they seemed to say.

At sunset the sky changed from orange and gold to dark blue and then a velvety black. It had been a long day. Tired to the bone, Anita went off to her bunk. As she snuggled down under a wool blanket, she could hear the spars creaking, and the wind whistling through the rigging.

In the middle of the night she woke up. Bright moonlight streaming through the porthole fell across her face. She wrapped the blanket around herself and stepped out on deck. It was almost as bright as day. The helmsman stood at the wheel holding the ship on course. A seaman stood forward in the bow keeping watch for small boats adrift, or other ships approaching from the south. Two other seamen on watch talked quietly on the left, or port side of the ship.

Anita walked across the deck to the opposite side and looked over the starboard rail at the dark waters swirling past. Suddenly a long dark shape came to the surface alongside the ship, just below where Anita stood. It was a huge gray whale, her hide all scarred and crusted with white barnacles. A young calf, as large as the longboat, rested half out of the water across his mother's back. Startled, Anita became aware of a large blue eye, the size of a dinner plate, studying her deliberately and unafraid. Anita stared back, locked eye to eye with the whale.

She seems so knowing. She seems to be looking right into my soul. Why, she is showing off her calf the way our black mare shows off a new foal. Anita and the whale looked at each other for a few long moments. Then the whale gave a deep sigh, slapped her tail, and sank with her calf to the depths below. Anita peered down, but there was no trace of the whale on the surface of the sea.

"What was that?" barked one of the seamen in Spanish as he ran to the starboard side of the ship.

"Only a big gray whale. She came up with her calf for a few minutes, and then dove right down again. It's all right. She wasn't angry or anything."

"Only a big gray whale," said the seaman. His face went white in the moonlight. "She could have stove a hole in the ship with that tail."

"She's gone now." Anita was annoyed that the seaman regarded the whale as threatening. She thought of the whale as a friendly female animal. Then she said to herself, he's deathly afraid of the whale, and I'm not. I was scared of that mountain lion on the Sespe, but I knew Lorenzo would take care of me. The thought of bats makes my skin crawl. She shivered at the memory. Pulling the blanket closer around herself, she returned to her bunk deep in thought. I was terrified when Don Ramón held that pistol to Father's head. I guess I'm just afraid of things and people I don't understand. She put her head down on the pillow and fell fast asleep.

Standing on the deck the next morning, Anita saw a great headland rise up out of the sea. The Spanish called it Point Loma because the headland looked like the back, or *loma,* of a huge steer lying down in a field. The *Pride of Nantucket* sailed around Point Loma and entered the beautiful harbor of San Diego. Captain Biddle guided his brig past the sandbar near the entrance and dropped the anchor a short distance from shore. Two ships, the *Alert* and the *Pilgrim* from Boston, lay at anchor some distance away.

The crew were excited and happy to see the other ships. They could row across the water and visit their friends from home. Two seamen manned the longboat and brought

Don José, Captain Biddle and Anita to the beach. A big, tall sailor picked up Anita and carried her to the dry, sandy beach so she would not get her feet wet.

"We leave for Santa Barbara the day after tomorrow," said Captain Biddle. "It will take four days to get back because we'll be sailing against the wind. I'll see you and Anita tomorrow evening at Don Juan Bandini's."

Don Juan Bandini was famous for his hospitality throughout California. "He is a distant cousin of ours," said Don José.

"His house is a few miles from here close to the *presidio*," said Captain Biddle. He waved his hand toward a wooden building up the beach. "You can rent horses there to ride to the Bandini home." He looked doubtfully at Anita. "The horses are a bit wild though."

Don José laughed. "My little *ranchera* can ride any horse that's broken to the saddle."

As they walked to the corral, Anita found it hard to keep her balance. Captain Biddle chuckled. "You're walking on sea legs as though you're still on a rolling ship. That means you are a real blue water sailor. You'll be all right when you get your land legs back again."

At the corral a man brought out two scrawny looking animals, not at all like the well groomed saddle horses of Rancho del Mar. Don José boosted Anita up in the saddle and shortened the stirrups so that she could put her feet in them.

"Don't worry about bringing the horses back," said their owner. "Turn them loose and they'll come back here by themselves."

Don José shook hands with Captain Biddle. "*Adiós*, my friend," he said. "We'll see you at Don Juan Bandini's."

As they rode to the Bandini house through the morning

sunshine, an amused and baffled Don José shook his head. "Anita, five days ago I took you along on an ordinary business trip to Santa Barbara. I never dreamed that we would find ourselves in San Diego, but I shouldn't be so surprised. Ordinary trips somehow become extraordinary when you come along."

FIESTA AT SAN DIEGO

*A*nita liked the Bandinis. Doña Refugio treated her like a daughter, and Don Juan acted like a kindly uncle. The Bandinis warmly welcomed their distant cousins from San Buenaventura. Don Juan lent a complete change of clothes to Don José. Anita wore a pretty flowered dress and a white petticoat that Josefa Bandini had outgrown. The clothes Anita and her father wore on the ship were handed to the maids to be washed and ironed.

"We must get you ready for the fiesta this evening," said Doña Refugio as she sat down in a chair by the big sunny window in the *sala*. Anita sat on a low stool in front of her. "While I brush your hair, I can watch the servants on the patio and the maids getting this room ready for our party tonight. Now, tell me, Anita, how are Francisca and Luisa?

I haven't seen them in so long, not since I lived in Santa Barbara, many years ago."

"Mother is fine," answered Anita. She is always busy running the ranch house. She sees that the servants weed and water the vegetable and herb gardens. She tells Beatriz, the cook, what to make for our meals and makes sure the *vaqueros* have plenty to eat. Mother tells the maids when to wash our clothes and when to sweep the house and patio. She sews all our clothes and somehow finds time to grow pretty flowers. Of course, Tía Luisa and María Isabel help her, but Mother keeps the house running properly."

Doña Refugio began to brush Anita's back curls. "What tangles the sea wind has put in your hair! How is Luisa? My, how she used to dance! When she and your father danced *el jarabe*, everyone else would stop dancing to watch. What fun she was, always playing tricks and telling jokes. Francisca told me once that when Luisa was a girl in Old Mexico, she used to think up all kinds of excuses to get out of the house. She loved to go riding around town in the carriage. 'I'm going to church,' she would say to her father. The church was always on the far side of town."

Anita had not known much about this side of Tía Luisa. Doña Refugio continued talking as she worked the hairbrush gently over Anita's dark curls. "Luisa could do beautiful embroidery when they got her to sit down long enough."

"She still embroiders beautifully. She embroidered the blouse I wore on the ship. She dances at all our fiestas. When everyone else is tired, she wants to keep on dancing. Because Mother is so busy with the house, Tía Luisa teaches us music, dancing and embroidery. Two *rancheros* proposed marriage to her but she says she likes to live with us. I always wondered why she left Mexico and came to

Rancho del Mar."

"My dear," said Doña Refugio, "you know that shortly after she married, her husband was killed by bandits. Such a sad thing to have happen. They loved each other so much. He was very rich and left Luisa all his property. The family tried to arrange another marriage for her, but she said she didn't want to marry again."

Anita sat quietly on the low chair. She knew that sometimes, if you sat quietly when adults were speaking, they often forgot you were there and spoke freely. She heard some interesting stories that way.

Doña Refugio picked up the comb and worked on a spot where the curls were tangled. She seemed to be talking aloud to herself. "The family wanted to control her property. They didn't care if she were happy or not. Only your father understood how she felt. She talked it over with him. He took Luisa to see the archbishop. Luisa said she wanted to build a home for orphan children. She signed over management of her property to the Sisters of Mercy keeping only a small part as income for herself. How angry the family was! They couldn't do anything because she had the archbishop on her side. She stayed until the home was finished and the orphans moved in. Then one day she quietly left for Acapulco where she boarded a ship for Santa Barbara. She arrived shortly after José's wedding to Francisca. That Luisa, so independent. She always did what she thought was right." Doña Refugio began brushing Anita's side curls. "Now, tell me about your brothers and your sister."

Anita smiled. She knew very well that all the California *rancheros* were interested in each other's children in order that suitable marriages could be arranged among the families. "María Isabel is sixteen and has three proposals of marriage already. Father says she is too young to get married, but Mother says that María Isabel can run a household as well as she herself can. Tonio is thirteen and helps at roundup time. He can throw a rope around anything that runs on four feet."

Doña Refugio laughed. "How are the terrible twins? Luisa wrote to me about them. They were always getting into things."

"They are eighteen years old now. Father is so proud of them. Enrique and Fernando are very good with horses. They have already raised some fine saddle horses on our ranch."

"And Lorenzo, he is your oldest brother, isn't he?" asked Doña Refugio as she brushed the last tangled curl.

"Father says Lorenzo has a good head for business, and he's teaching him how to trade with the sea captains and merchants in Santa Barbara."

Doña Refugio sighed. "My husband and I had hoped our young cousin would go into the hide trade. We even hired a tutor for Felix, but he has not been a good student."

Suddenly there was a loud crash outside and an angry exchange of words between two servants. Doña Refugio walked outside to find a large jar shattered in pieces on the patio, a manservant soaked from head to foot with water, a pile of clean clothes scattered on the ground, and a maid holding her head in pain. "Why don't you look where you're going?" she cried out angrily.

"You're supposed to get out of my way when I'm carrying the heavy *olla* filled with water. Now look what you've done! It will take me another hour to draw up enough water from the well," said the manservant, mopping his face.

"Felisa," said Doña Refugio calmly to the maid, "Bring

the clean clothes that are still dry into the house and hang the others in the sunlight. Ricardo, pick up the broken clay pieces and throw them away. Find another large *olla* and fill it so that there will be plenty of water on hand for the fiesta tonight. Make sure we have plenty of torches around the wall of the patio so that we'll have enough light."

The noise had brought all the other servants out of the house.They quickly went back to their chores when Doña Refugio waved them all inside. Josefa and her cousin, Felix, came out to the patio. "Mother, I want to see if my yellow fiesta dress fits Anita." She turned to her cousin from San Buenaventura and said, "The party tonight will be fun. Only fifty people though, but we'll have *cascarones*."

"What are *cascarones?*" Anita thought they were something to eat.

Felix laughed. "You don't know what *cascarones* are? You'll find out tonight. By the way," he said in a bored tone, "there'll be a traveling Spanish circus at the party. You'll probably enjoy the show. Thank goodness there'll be plenty of dancing. Do you know how to dance?"

"Of course," said Anita, adding silently to herself, I've been taught by an expert.

"What is it like up north where you live? Do you see many wild Indians up there?" asked thirteen-year-old Felix in a superior manner.

"Why, yes, we do," answered Anita coolly. "A few years ago a band of desert Indians attacked San Buenaventura Mission to steal away the Indian girls. It was Sunday morning and we were all in church. Our soldiers and the *rancheros* killed several and chased the rest back to the desert. Once in a while a few come back and hang around, but they don't give any trouble. When we're in church, we always have to put a guard on the horses though." To herself she said, he thinks I'm just a country girl who doesn't know how to dance and doesn't know what *cascarones* are. I'll show him.

Josefa took Anita's hand and led the way to the storeroom where she opened chests and boxes until she found the fiesta dress she was looking for. Anita gasped in delight. It was a lovely yellow Chinese silk and there were dancing slippers to match. "It's beautiful," breathed Anita. "Where did you find the silk, in Mexico?"

"Oh, no." Josefa smiled. "By moonlighting, of course."

"What is moonlighting?" Anita wanted to know.

"You know that Spain used to forbid us to trade with the Yankee and English ships. The ships would anchor out in the harbor, and on bright, moonlit nights the sailors would row us from shore out to the ships where we could buy all sorts of lovely things that we couldn't get from Old Mexico. The captains would sell us silks from China, velvets, and perfumes from Europe, calico cottons, needles and scissors from England, and all kinds of books, tools and iron goods from the United States. We exchanged cattle hides for everything we needed or wanted without having to pay any taxes to Spain. There still are no stores in San Diego where Mother and I can go shopping. We order through the ships' agents.

Quickly Josefa put the fiesta dress over Anita's head and pulled it down. It was a perfect fit and so were the slippers. "You'll look so pretty at the fiesta tonight. My father used to call me Miss Sunflower when I wore this dress. Here, let me show you my doll." She pulled a carefully wrapped little bundle from a box and showed Anita the doll.

"She is wearing a dress of the same yellow silk," said Anita.

"Yes, I keep her because I may have a little girl some day who will love her as much as I do. Her name is Girasol."

Josefa gently packed away her doll in the storage box and closed the lid carefully. She folded the yellow silk dress over her arm saying, "I'll ask Lupe to press this for you. Now, we are almost ready for the fiesta. We still have to make the *cascarones*. Come, we'll fix them out on the porch in the shade."

Josefa called her maid who took away the silk dress to press out the creases. Then Josefa led Anita to the kitchen. Opening the cupboards, she gathered up a supply of beeswax, a candle, a flask of perfume marked "Attar of Roses, Hungary," and a basket of eggshells.

"Now we are ready to begin." Josefa set the supplies down on a table in the shade. "Here, you can see that these eggshells are hollow with a hole at one end. I'll put some rose perfume inside and seal it up with a little melted beeswax. In Mexico they cut colored paper into tiny pieces called confetti to put inside, but we use perfume. Tonight at the party, we'll play a game. You are supposed to break the eggshell over somebody's head and run away before the person sees you. Of course, everyone else is trying to do the same thing to you. It's fun."

"I'm going to try to hit Captain Biddle." Anita chuckled. "He's so serious."

"My father and your father have been in the office all day talking business with Captain Biddle," said Josefa. "Come, it's getting warm, time to take a long nap before the fiesta tonight. Let's go to my room where it's cool."

When Anita woke up, it was dark outside. The pretty yellow dress, neatly pressed, hung over a chair. Josefa put on a green silk dress with a beautiful lace collar and a green velvet sash. She fastened a white blossom in her hair and turned to smile down at Anita.

"Our guests are arriving. The Estudillo and Lopez families are already here. I'll help you put on your dress and tie the velvet sash. Here is a pair of white silk stockings. Your dancing slippers are under the chair."

After putting on the dress and slippers, Anita peeked at her reflection in the long mirror. I do look nice, she said to herself. Grown up.

They went outside to the patio where food and drink were set out on long tables among the green plants and bright flowers that were Doña Refugio's pride and joy. It was a starry San Diego night. Around the patio walls, blazing torches had been set firmly in special holders to give plenty of light. A warm, gentle breeze from Mexico blew through the big olive tree in the center of the patio. Anita inspected the platters of meat and fruit. Just like home, she thought, but the fruit is different. She saw papayas and guavas that did not grow along San Buenaventura's cool coast. "Where do they come from?" she asked Josefa.

"The padres grow the fruit in a nearby canyon where the climate is as sunny and warm as tropical Mexico."

Anita found her father in the patio with Captain Biddle. They were talking to a small dark-eyed man with a gold earring in his ear. He was a Spanish gypsy and the owner of the traveling circus. The circus had just arrived from Monterey in northern California. While the gypsy reported the latest news from the capital, Don José listened with a thoughtful expression on his face. Captain looked alert and interested as he jabbed questions to the man about names and dates and places.

When Anita approached, Captain Biddle pretended not to recognize her in the borrowed yellow silk dress. "Who is this little Miss Sunflower?" he asked in his correct Spanish.

"Allow me to present my daughter to you, sir," said Anita's father proudly.

Anita felt her cheeks burn, then she curtsied and said, "Come into the *sala*. In a few minutes, Josefa is going to dance '*El Son.*' "

A hundred beeswax candles flamed in iron sconces fixed to the walls. Beeswax candles, not the smoky tallow kind we use, thought Anita as she walked through the doorway. How expensive! The Bandinis certainly know how to give a party.

The long, narrow *sala* had been cleared of sofas and tables. Silver mirrors reflected flickering candles and glistening silks. The ladies and girls sat in chairs placed along the walls. Young *rancheros* in short jackets, red cummerbunds, and wide-bottomed trousers with silver buttons down the side-seams eyed the girls who wore dresses of every color of the rainbow. Anita sat down beside Doña Refugio as the orchestra of three violins and three guitars began to play a slow dance tune.

Don Juan Bandini proudly led Josefa to the middle of the floor, set a silken white rope at her feet and a glass of water on her head. Anita had never before seen a dance like this one. Alone in the center of the floor, Josefa moved slowly and gracefully to the music as she balanced the glass of water on her head. She stepped carefully in and around the rope, feeling with the toe of her slipper. When the music stopped, the silk rope was tied into a love knot and the glass of water remained unspilled on the top of her head. As the guests clapped enthusiastically, Don Juan led Josefa back to her chair and the orchestra struck up a lively *el jarabe* tune.

Anita was still clapping for Josefa when Felix stood before her and asked, "Would Señorita Sunflower let me have the honor of dancing with her?"

Carefully keeping a straight face, Anita went out on the dance floor. Now we'll see who knows how to dance, she said to herself, as she and Felix joined the couples tapping their feet.

Felix led Anita through a series of difficult steps. He was rather surprised that his partner followed him so easily. He tried a few more steps, more difficult than the others. Anita followed, her slippered feet never missing a beat. Then Felix stood still for an instant. Immediately Anita took the lead and moved into Tía Luisa's special step that left Felix breathless trying to keep up.

"Where did you learn that step?"

"Oh," said Anita casually, "everybody in Santa Barbara knows it." She was too kind to say that her twin brothers could ride horses and rope cattle all day, then come home, clean up, change clothes and dance that step all night at a party. Somehow she could not imagine Felix riding horses and roping cattle all day.

"You really can dance," said Felix in admiration. "I'll have to learn that step," he said as she twirled around him under his arm.

Anita knew that she had made her point and, because she did not want to be impolite, she complimented Felix on his graceful dancing. He led her back to her seat next to Doña Refugio who was applauding them.

"Anita, you are so much like Luisa."

"Do you really think so?" Anita smiled. "She has spent hours teaching María Isabel and me how to dance."

"The next dance is for the young people," said Doña Refugio as a dozen girls in colorful dresses moved out across the floor twisting and turning gracefully in time to the music. Nearby a young *ranchero* reached out as a girl turned away from him and clapped his hat on her head. "If she keeps his hat on, he will be her partner this evening." The girl tossed her head and the hat fell on the floor. The red-faced young *ranchero* picked it up while his friends hooted and made fun of him. A few minutes later the same young *ranchero* found a pretty girl who kept his hat on her head.

Doña Refugio's eyes searched the floor for Josefa. She looked approvingly at her daughter's partner, the son of a wealthy landowner. Then she said, "Luisa told me that when Francisca was dancing, she always seemed to recognize José's hat although she never saw him put it on her head. We always wondered how she could tell."

"Oh, don't you know?" Anita chuckled. It was her turn to tell a secret. "Father always kept his best hat in a box with rosemary leaves. When the hat on her head smelled of rosemary, Mother always knew it belonged to Father."

"Imagine that, rosemary," said her hostess. "Rosemary. That reminds me. I want to send your mother some flower and herb seeds and some cuttings from our new rosebush. She would probably like some cuttings of the *flor de nochebuena*, too. Don't let me forget to give them to you before you leave tomorrow."

"I won't," promised Anita. "When do we throw the *cascarones*?"

"After the circus show," said Doña Refugio.

There was an excited shout from the patio and much noisy clapping. The circus performers took their places. Everyone crowded outside. The whole neighborhood seemed to be hanging over the patio walls. In the doorways local Indians stretched their necks to see the show.

First came the acrobats, leaping over each other, and turning cartwheels and somersaults in the air. There was a little trick dog that jumped through a fiery hoop. A funny monkey wearing a red cap and jacket drove a wagon drawn by a little white goat. They gave the dog a ride around the patio. A knife thrower followed. He threw knives all around a pretty girl who was standing in front of a wide board. The last act was a gypsy girl about Anita's age who danced a lively *flamenco* from southern Spain. The guests clapped, whistled shrilly, and stamped their feet. The applause was deafening.

Then the monkey came around through the crowd holding out his little red cap. He came up to Anita and she dropped a shelled walnut into his cap. The monkey picked it out of his cap and chattered angrily at her. She drew back, afraid he would bite. "Here, Anita, give him this," said Don Juan's voice over her shoulder. "He wants a coin, not a walnut."

Anita looked at the silver coin he placed in her hand. She had never handled money before. While she was looking curiously at the coin, the monkey sprang up, grabbed the coin from her hand and jumped down, scolding her all the while.

From the *sala* came the sound of laughter and music. Anita went back inside to watch the fun. Josefa crept up behind her and squished an eggshell on her head. Anita laughed and sat down beside Doña Refugio. All around the room girls and their partners were breaking *cascarones* over the heads of their friends. Anita noticed that the most popular girls had the most eggshells in their hair. Doña Refugio brought out some *cascarones* from a basket under her chair and gave them to Anita. She took one and looked around for Captain Biddle. He was seated on a chair talking to Josefa. Anita slipped through the crowd, cracked a *cascarón* on his head and was away before he could tell who did it. This was a game she played like an expert. She caught her father by surprise and almost, but not quite, caught Josefa. Anita cracked one over Felix's head. He took it with good humor, but never knew who hit him. She went back to sit by Doña Refugio. The music had changed and so had the dance.

"It's a waltz," explained her hostess, "from Vienna, a one, two, three, one, two, three beat. Sometimes the music is very fast. Couples face each other. The man places his right hand around the lady's waist and holds up her right hand in his left hand. As he leads his partner across the floor, he turns them around in a circle. Here comes Mr. O'Leary to ask me to dance."

A pleasant young man with reddish brown hair and lively green eyes approached Doña Refugio. Speaking in clear Castilian Spanish, he asked her to dance. "*Encantada* (I would be delighted), *señor*," replied Doña Refugio.

Anita sat by herself for only a moment. Felix appeared and asked her to dance. "I don't know how to waltz," she said.

"I'll teach you."

Before Anita realized it, she was gliding across the floor with Felix. She liked the waltz because she could talk as she danced. She noticed the whole dance floor was buzzing with conversation.

Felix said, "The *padres* think the waltz is shocking, but everybody is dancing it. The waltz started in Vienna and spread all over Europe and, of course, came to Mexico. In fact, it was my cousin, Don Juan Bandini, who brought the waltz from Mexico to San Diego."

"Who is Mr. O'Leary?" asked Anita as they whirled

over the polished floor.

"He is my tutor," said Felix. "But he's leaving soon. The sooner the better. What a bore! Books, books, books. He expects me to read one a week. Can you imagine anything more dull?"

"Where is he from?" she asked. "He speaks Spanish with a different accent."

"I know he came out from Philadelphia in the United States," said Felix, expertly turning away from a plump *ranchero* couple about to crash into them. "He trained for the law there. He was ready to go into practice when the girl he planned to marry died of a fever. He was heartbroken. He felt very ill for a long time and when he recovered, he decided to go off to California to forget. He's rather a nice fellow, but I certainly don't need to know all those things he tries to teach me, mathematics, Latin, English, rhetoric and all that stuff."

"Why? What makes you think you won't need it?"

"Don Juan Bandini is my godfather and when I am eighteen, he will arrange a nice position for me here in the San Diego Customs Office. No doubt Don Juan will be given a high office under our new governor. Haven't you heard the news? Everybody is talking about it."

"What news?" asked Anita.

"The circus owner, that Spanish gypsy who just arrived from Monterey, told Don Juan today that Governor Mariano Chico is operating according to Mexican law rather than California custom. All cargo must land at Monterey. No retail trade on board foreign ships. The Spanish *padres* must leave or swear to be loyal to the government of Mexico. The governor will take charge of all the mission lands in Alta California and will lease them to whoever has enough money to pay the price. The *padres* will be in charge of church affairs only. Don Juan has good friends in high places so our family should do very well."

Anita was troubled. "Under Spanish law the mission lands and the cattle rightfully belong to the Mission Indians. If San Buenaventura Mission is secularized like the rest, and their land rights taken away, where will the Christian Indians go? What will they do for food? Those Chumash in the *rancherías* are starving now."

"Oh, they'll manage by themselves," said Felix casually. "We are no longer ruled by Spain. Mexico is making its own laws now, and we *californios* are governed by Mexico."

The waltz ended and Felix escorted Anita back to her chair where they met Doña Refugio and Mr. O'Leary. Felix asked his godmother to dance the next waltz. Mr. O'Leary smiled at Anita and said, "Would you like to dance, *señorita* ?"

"*Encantada*," replied Anita in her best fiesta manner. To herself she thought, if I keep him talking, maybe he won't step on my feet. Mr. O'Leary turned out to be a good waltzer. Anita asked politely, "Where do you come from, *señor* ?"

"I was born in Bandon, County Cork. That's in Ireland where the land is very green. I learned my languages at the university in Dublin and practiced them in Europe."

"Felix said you lived in Philadelphia in the United States."

"Yes, I became a lawyer there, but one cold, cold winter I caught pneumonia and, when I was well, I sailed for California. They told me it would be warm and sunny here. Where are you from, *señorita* ?"

"Please call me Anita. Everyone does. We live up north near Mission San Buenaventura on Rancho Santa Cruz del

Mar, or as we say, Rancho del Mar. It is a little cooler there than in San Diego, but Father says it's the best climate in the world."

"I've been thinking it's time to leave San Diego and visit somewhere else. I'm one of those Irishmen who like to travel."

"Please come to visit us at Rancho del Mar. You would like it there."

The waltz ended and Mr. O'Leary escorted Anita back to her chair.

Felix was waiting for her and said, "Are you thirsty, Anita? Would you like a *refresco*? They have just brought out a bowl of my favorite kind."

Mr. O'Leary excused himself and sat down by Doña Refugio. Anita said, "Yes, I would like something to drink. I'm thirsty."

Felix escorted Anita to the table where a servant poured cool *refresco* into glasses. A thin, sharp-faced girl, who had been flirting with two blond brothers from behind her fan, came over as Felix handed Anita a glass of the cool fruit punch.

"Herlinda, have you met Anita Lorenzana?" asked Felix. "Anita, this is Herlinda Cuen. Her father is a captain in the Mexican Army."

The two girls took each other's measure. Herlinda's eyes narrowed as she looked Anita up and down with deliberate slowness. Herlinda could not find any fault in the hair arrangement, the silk dress, or the silk stockings and satin slippers. Her lips curled in a small smile. Herlinda's hair was slicked down with a heavy coat of oil. It was crusted here and there with eggshell fragments. She could use a good shampoo, thought Anita.

"May I also present Domingo Santos and his brother

Rafael who are visiting us from Mexico City?" Two pairs of cold gray eyes appraised her. She noted they combed their short blond hair high over the forehead in the latest Mexico City style.

Anita smiled at the three strangers. "How do you do. I am visiting from San Buenaventura." The well-dressed Santos brothers exchanged a knowing glance. They bowed and studied her intently with tight, shrewd smiles.

"O-ooh!" trilled Herlinda, "You must be the little *ranchera* they were talking about. Whatever do you do all day on the ranch?" she asked, smirking and sliding her eyes around to Rafael and Domingo. "Do you rope cattle and shoot grizzly bears?"

What have I done to deserve this? Anita asked herself. This little pussycat is ready to claw me. She answered with a dignified smile, "Yes, I have shot at a bear, but I prefer to leave the grizzlies to my brothers. There are so many other things to do. I have my lessons, my music, and my embroidery." She was determined to hide her annoyance from the obnoxious girl.

Herlinda trilled again. "Felix says there are wild Indians up there. How do you stand it, living way out in the country like that?"

"We like it very much," replied the little *ranchera* in a level tone. She knew she was being made fun of and did not like it.

Then Domingo, the eighteen-year-old brother, suddenly entered the conversation and asked with lively interest, "Are you related to the Lorenzanas of Mexico City?"

"Yes," answered Anita. "They are my first cousins."

Rafael, who was thirteen, glanced at his brother and raised his eyebrows like a pair of signal flags. "The

97

Lorenzanas are almost as wealthy as the Torals."

"My mother is Francisca Toral," answered Anita in the same even tone. She was learning to play their game, but she did not like it at all.

Herlinda's expression changed from disdain to a grudging respect when she learned Anita's family connections. Then she fluttered her fan and said sweetly, "Felix, be a dear and dance this waltz with me."

She stole my next dance, fumed Anita while Felix's eyes begged for forgiveness over Herlinda's shoulder.

"May I have this dance, *señorita* ?" asked Domingo.

"Yes, indeed," replied Anita. They waltzed smoothly across the floor, leaving Rafael to gorge on candied fruit.

"Is your father's ranch a large one?" inquired Domingo.

"Large enough," answered Anita.

"Felix says you have a sister. Is she older or younger than you?"

"She is sixteen." Anita thought, really, this fellow's questions are too prying and personal. I don't like to chat with him. His manners are perfect, but his smile is insincere.

"My brother and I are going to live on a ranch near San Buenaventura," said Domingo. "My uncle, Teodoro Valencia, owns Rancho del Agua Dulce. In fact he has plans to acquire more land nearby."

Anita was careful to keep her face blank. He does, does he? Is he talking about the Quintero rancho, or the mission land, or our land? Father will want to know about this. Aloud she remarked, "Rancho del Agua Dulce is on the other side of the hills from ours." She changed the subject. "Does Herlinda live in San Diego?"

"Yes, her father is a military officer on temporary duty here. She didn't want to leave Mexico City." Domingo seemed to be ready to ask more questions, but the waltz ended. Anita thanked him graciously and sat down on an empty chair by Josefa. Domingo bowed politely and went back to his brother. He's going to tell his brother everything he learned from me, thought Anita. She saw a tall, thin man in a gray suit join the brothers at the punch bowl and listen attentively to Domingo.

Josefa nudged Anita's arm with her elbow and looked across the room. "Herlinda has done it again." In the far corner of the *sala*, a young girl wearing a light blue dress suddenly burst into tears. She abruptly broke away from the group of young people. "Herlinda is always making cutting remarks to the lieutenant's daughter, always pulling rank. Look, now Herlinda has accidentally on purpose spilled punch down the front of the Estudillo girl's new red silk dress. That spoiled Cuen girl is impossible tonight."

"Why does she act that way?" Anita wanted to know. She could hear Herlinda's voice trilling from across the room.

"She has no mother to teach her manners. Her father and their servants have thoroughly spoiled her. She can't stand not being the center of attention. She seems to be happiest when she can make someone cry."

A young *ranchero* came up to Josefa and asked her to dance. Anita sat alone for a moment. Then a mischievous smile turned up the corners of her mouth. Hmm, Herlinda likes to be the center of attention, does she?

Anita picked up Josefa's basket of *cascarones* and slipped out a side door. She walked quietly along the path to the kitchen and opened the door. The room was empty. I'm certain I'll find some in here. Sure enough, the Bandini's cook stored eggs in a basket in the cupboard, just as Beatriz did. Anita picked up a large brown egg from the basket and placed it gently on top of the white *cascarones*. She thought, that way I'll know which egg to choose.

She returned to the brightly lit *sala*. Placing the basket under her chair, Anita joined the laughing crowd breaking *cascarones* over unsuspecting heads. Anita moved quickly through the dancers, passing behind Herlinda. "Plop!" The egg broke in a gummy mess over Herlinda's head. There was an outraged shriek, but Anita was already on the other side of the room. She sat down by Doña Refugio and watched the dancing couples.

"Did you see that?" asked Felix, reaching in the basket for more *cascarones*. "Someone squashed a real egg over Herlinda's hair. She's so mad. Her father is taking her home. Everyone is laughing and wishing they had done it. It was a spoiled egg, too. She really has been asking for it tonight."

"Something like that was bound to happen. She has been going out of her way to say mean, catty things to people," said Doña Refugio.

Anita sniffed, suddenly aware that there was a trace of rotten egg yolk on her right hand. She picked up a *cascarón* and crushed it in her hand. The perfume dripped through her fingers. She turned to Don José who was standing behind her with Captain Biddle. "May I borrow your handkerchief, Father? It's hard to get the perfume off my hand."

Anita looked up at her father innocently. Don José looked down his long nose at her and said, "Yes, I imagine that yellow perfume is very hard to wipe off." His green eyes crinkled with laughter and his mouth turned up at the corners as he gave her his handkerchief.

Anita carefully wiped her hands on the white linen square. She did not dare look at her father, or she would have laughed out loud. He saw me. I know he did, she said to herself.

Don José said, "It's time for us to leave. We must go to bed now because we get up early tomorrow morning to return to the ship."

His daughter turned away to look again at the dance floor. Josefa was breaking a *cascarón* over Mister O'Leary's head. Anita laughed out loud and then felt a "squish" on her own head. A drop of rose perfume trickled down her neck. She turned around quickly. Her father and Captain Biddle had stopped talking and seemed to be watching the dancers. Nearby Doña Refugio laughed and shook her head. She wouldn't tell Anita who had thrown the *cascarón*. Anita knew it hadn't been her father.

"I must leave now, too," said Captain Biddle. "I have a report to write to the shipowners about the news from Monterey and all the changes that will take place in California under Governor Chico. If the wind is right, the *Alert* sails tomorrow morning for Boston. If I write my report tonight, I can give it to the captain before the *Alert* weighs anchor." He said good night to Don José and Anita, and thanked Doña Refugio for her hospitality.

Later, tucked between warm blankets with a soft pillow under her head, Anita's mind whirled with all sorts of thoughts. The Bandinis are large landowners. We own land, too, but not as much. The Bandinis seem to be rich. They give splendid parties and buy expensive items from the traders like rose perfume from Hungary, beeswax candles, velvets and silks. The Bandinis have many servants. Josefa even has a personal maid. We have servants, too, but not as many, except at roundup time when we hire about a hundred *vaqueros* and extra cooks to feed them. That Herlinda is such a pill. Josefa says Domingo Santos cashed in his inheritance and came to California looking for a wealthy wife. Did Captain Biddle break that last *cascarón* over my head? How could I possibly have known that brown egg was rotten?

Anita finally drifted off to sleep dreaming that she was waltzing by herself with a glass of water on her head and the monkey was chasing her around the patio hitting her with eggshells.

THE YANKEE PASSENGER

*A*rre! Arre! (Get moving!)." The driver's whip cracked in the cool morning air. The yoked oxen strained forward, muscles rippling under their glossy hides like molten silver. The huge wooden wheels creaked through the dust toward the harbor. Don José and Mr. O'Leary rode alongside the *carreta*. Half-hidden among the soft pillows, Anita clutched a bulging wicker satchel and listened.

"Don Juan told me that you have experience teaching in a young gentlemen's school in Dublin," said Don José.

"Yes, sir. I taught a few classes there while I was studying at the university."

"Then you taught classes in mathematics, history and languages to young people the same age as my children?"

"Yes, sir," replied Mr. O'Leary. "Don Juan said you

needed a tutor for your children. I am looking for a new position."

Don José began to talk about the lack of schools in California. When they reached the landing place at the beach, Mr. O'Leary swung down from his saddle and helped Anita out of the *carreta*. Just as if I were grown up, she thought.

Don José made a quick decision. "If you are looking for a new position, why not come to Rancho del Mar and tutor my children?"

"Agreed, sir." They shook hands. "As soon as my Mexican citizenship papers arrive, I'll leave immediately for Santa Barbara."

"Very well, we will be expecting you at Rancho del Mar in a few weeks."

"*Hasta la vista*," said Mr. O'Leary to Anita.

"*Adiós, señor*," replied Anita as she picked up her satchel and walked across the sand. She saw that the brig *Alert* was still lying at anchor out in the harbor. A short distance away on the beach, a man was shouting and waving by a large pile of luggage.

Two sailors from the *Pride of Nantucket* waited in the longboat. They paid no attention to the man. They stood up as Anita and her father walked toward them. The boat bobbed gently in the water. One bare-legged, tattooed sailor jumped out and waded to the sandy beach. He picked her up, waded back through the water, and carefully set Anita and her wicker satchel safely in the boat.

He returned to the beach where he and the other sailor balanced Don José on their shoulders, carried him to the longboat, and set him down beside Anita. Because there was no pier, passengers had to be carried to the longboats. The sailors hauled in the light anchor and pulled on the oars with care so that Anita and her father were not splashed with cold salt water. The man with the luggage stamped his feet and shouted after them.

As they rowed out to the *Pride of Nantucket*, Anita noticed that the air was still and warm, the water was calm and white, puffy clouds moved slowly across the blue sky. She felt the sudden touch of a cool northwest wind on her face. When they rowed past the *Alert*, Anita heard the first mate call out, "Topmen, lay aloft and loose royals and t'gallants."

Sailors ran out quickly along the high spars to unreef the sails while other seamen pushed on the wheel of the capstan to hoist the anchor. In a loud chorus they sang, "Time for us to go," as the anchor rose to the catshead. A sailor raised the long, red and white, homeward bound pennant to the top of the tall foremast. They were on their way home, but it would be five months before the *Alert* saw Boston again.

From the huts on the beach where the cattle hides had been stored, the Kanaka sailors from the Sandwich Islands were singing goodbye to their friends on the *Alert*. Led by a man with a high falsetto voice, the song sounded both beautiful and sad at the same time, as if the men were singing with tears in their eyes. The Kanakas sang until the *Alert* rounded Point Loma and sailed out of sight.

Anita climbed the ladder to the *Pride's* deck and looked for Paolo. She found him in his usual place near the mainmast and sat down beside him on a big coil of rope. "What were those men singing, Paolo? They kept saying the word '*Aloha*' again and again."

"That's the way they say farewell whenever someone leaves the Islands. '*Aloha*' means both 'Hello' and 'Goodbye until we meet again.'"

"*Aloha*," she repeated. "I like that word."

At the gangway Captain Biddle greeted Don José with a friendly handshake, saying, "You came at just the right time. We'll be leaving shortly. Another passenger is waiting on the beach. After we pick him up we must take advantage of the northwest wind to get the ship underway as soon as possible."

Anita put away her satchel in the Captain's cabin and returned to the railing. The longboat was approaching from the beach, two sailors straining at the oars. The boat rode low in the water although it carried only one passenger and his luggage. When the longboat came alongside the ship's ladder, there was an angry shout and a loud thumping.

She looked over the rail and saw a tall, thin man struggling to grab the bottom rung of the ladder. Again the longboat bumped the side of the brig. The man lost his balance and fell back awkwardly in the boat. He struggled upright and made a second try at grabbing the ladder. A sailor standing in the bow of the longboat shifted his weight from one leg to the other. Is he deliberately rocking the boat, Anita asked herself.

The passenger grabbed the ladder, but the longboat moved away again, leaving the passenger stretched out over the water. He held the last rung in a tight grip. His feet were still in the longboat. The sailors' faces showed no expression. They seemed to be carved out of wood. There was a loud splash and another angry shout. The sailors moved the longboat alongside the ladder.

Mr. Starbuck walked over to the gangway and looked down. "Reeve that line through the block," he ordered. A deckhand pulled a length of heavy rope over a pulley. Mr. Starbuck tossed the rope end down the ladder. "Tie this line around your waist, sir. We'll hoist you up. You two men there, lend a hand and haul on that line."

The deck hands hauled on the line and grinned at each other. They began to huff and puff as if the man were too heavy to lift. "Lend a hand here, mates," said one. Two more men joined them hauling on the line. One started to sing a sea chantey as if they were hoisting a heavy anchor. "Ho-oh-heave-ho!"

Anita saw Mr. Starbuck hide a smile behind his hand. Why was the crew making fun of the passenger, she wondered.

The sailors continued to huff and puff as they hoisted the man to the deck like a side of beef. At last the passenger appeared at the top of the gangway, sputtering in anger. He was soaking wet from head to foot and his fine silk coat was ripped up the back seam.

Why, he's all gray, thought Anita. Gray eyes, gray hair, gray skin, gray suit. All gray, except for his black boots. Didn't I see him at the fiesta last night? Of course, he was with the Santos brothers.

A young, blond, blue-eyed sailor clambered up the ship's ladder with the easy grace of an athlete. He handed the passenger his tall beaver hat. "It fell in the water, sir. It should be as good as new when it dries, I hope." His innocent choir boy look gave him away to Anita. It was the same look the twins wore when they were pulling off a practical joke.

The passenger grabbed his dripping hat. "Blundering incompetents! You clumsy oafs can't even row straight." He turned and shouted down the ladder. "Now bring my bags and boxes on board. Be careful with that cask of pickled peaches." The man's gray face had changed to a dark red. His pale gray eyes glared at Mr. Starbuck. "I'll report this to the owners, of that you may be sure."

Captain Biddle came forward and asked in a cool, quiet voice, "Are you Mr. Slope?"

"I am Samuel Slope of the Boston Slopes. I want you to discipline those men for not handling the longboat properly. My clothes are ruined! Why did those louts make me wait for the second boat? They took a man and a girl on board first."

Captain Biddle did not answer. His blue eyes were cold as Arctic ice. Turning to the young blond sailor, he spoke in what Anita called his captain-of-the-ship voice. "Billy, take Mr. Slope and his gear to the passenger's cabin." To the first mate, he said, "Mr. Starbuck, we must take advantage of the wind. We have lost too much time as it is. Secure the longboat. Make ready to raise the anchor and get underway."

Like the first mate of the *Alert*, Mr. Starbuck called out, "Topmen, lay aloft. Loose royals, t'gallants and topsails."

The crew sailed the ship out of the harbor with the skill of long practice. As she heard Mr. Starbuck calling out commands, Anita recalled how Tomás gave orders to the *vaqueros* at roundup time. Both men knew their jobs and did them well. Then she said to herself, Captain Biddle runs his ship the way Father runs the *rancho*.

The *Pride of Nantucket* sailed slowly past the sandbar at the harbor entrance. Anita looked back at the little town of San Diego. She thought about the fiesta of the night before. That morning Felix had seemed really sorry to see her leave. "It's a lot more fun when you're here," he said.

That evening Mr. Slope, in a dry set of gray clothes, joined Anita, her father, and the captain at dinner. He said very few words and those were in English to the cook. He spooned some pickled peaches for himself from a special dish, but he did not offer them to anyone else. What bad manners he has, she thought.

While eating dinner, Don José and Captain Biddle began talking about Governor Mariano Chico and the changes that would take place in California. "I wonder," said Don José, "who will benefit by this shift in the political winds?"

"Probably Don Juan Bandini," answered Anita as she poured herself a second cup of tea.

Both men looked at her curiously. Captain Biddle's fork stopped in mid-air. He put it down carefully and asked, "How do you know, Anita?"

"Who told you that?" asked her father.

"Felix," answered Anita. "He says he won't have to study anymore because his godfather has promised him a position in the Customs Service. Felix expects that the family will become very rich. They have many important friends in California and Mexico. Don Juan doesn't believe that Governor Chico will stay long in California. Don Juan thinks Los Angeles should be the capital instead of Monterey."

Captain Biddle and Don José exchanged meaningful looks. Anita saw Mr. Slope take a little book from his pocket and jot down something. He kept his eyes on his plate and did not look at anyone.

Don José's face showed concern. "If the politicians from Mexico can regulate trade along the coast and lease the Mission lands to anyone they please, what's to stop them from taking over the land commissions granted by the King of Spain?"

"Do you have papers proving Doña Francisca's legal right to Rancho del Mar?" asked Captain Biddle.

"Yes, I keep them in a special place in the house," said Don José.

"When I was in Monterey last year," the captain replied, "they told me that forty years ago the Californians did not mark their land grant boundaries precisely. They used for markers such things as oak trees that were later struck by lightning, or were cut up for firewood and hauled away. They often used stream beds that have since dried up, or cow skulls that have been covered by layers of mud and dead grass. Instead of metal chains, leather *reatas* were used to measure distance. Of course the leather would stretch in damp or rainy weather and shrink when it was dry. I hope your boundaries are more exact, my friend."

"Rancho Santa Cruz del Mar is marked by natural boundaries: the ocean, the Santa Clara River, and the hills to the east and north. However, it would do no harm to have the boundaries of the land commission measured exactly. What I need is a surveyor like your first president, George Washington."

"What is a surveyor?" asked Anita. Mr. Slope was writing rapidly in his book.

"A surveyor is a man who measures land areas across long distances," said Don José.

"He is something like a navigator," added Captain Biddle. "Instead of measuring distances over water, he measures distances on land. He uses some of the same tools."

"This unexpected trip to San Diego has been a good thing after all," said Don José. "How else would I have known about the need to survey the ranch? I know now that we Californians must use an English speaking agent in order to do business with American and British ships. Most of the goods we receive from Mexico come overland by muleback, and it is often broken or spoiled by rough handling. The *padres* tell me that it takes years to receive the things ordered from Mexico. The few pieces that come by Mexican ships are very expensive."

"I have seen some ships from Mexico anchored at Monterey and Santa Barbara," replied the captain. "Not many though."

"Yes," agreed Don José, "there are also a few from South America. We Californians prefer to buy from American or British ships because their prices are lower and their goods of higher quality. I wish they would land off San Buenaventura."

"The surf is very high there. Maybe some day someone will build a long pier, and then ships will be able to tie up and unload cargo."

"Well, my children are going to be prepared for that day. More and more American and British ships are coming to California. That's why I have arranged to hire Mr. O'Leary as a tutor. They need to learn English, history, mathematics and geography."

"Father, that will be wonderful!" exclaimed Anita. "I like Mr. O'Leary. I hope he will teach me English and French, too."

"A fine idea," said Captain Biddle. "My daughter, Martha, enjoys her French lessons and likes to test me on history. She asks me who Princess Victoria Alexandrina is, or who was Julius Caesar, or where the battle of Waterloo took place."

Don José looked carefully at Anita. He had not really planned to have his daughters tutored. "Would you like to learn about things like that?"

"It would be fun, Father, because Mr. O'Leary would make it interesting."

"How do you think María Isabel would feel about this?"

"She's very quick at numbers," said Anita. "I'm sure she

would do very well."

"All right, that question is settled then," said Don José. "I hope it will be as easy to solve the problems we *rancheros* have under these Mexican governors. The trouble is they send us men who want to rule, not govern."

Mr. Slope sipped his tea. He had filled several pages with notes. He was still writing when Anita left the captain's cabin and walked about on deck. Suddenly she heard a familiar sound, a sound she had not expected to hear on a ship. She heard it again and walked forward. "Ba-aa, ba-aa." On the fore hatch were several sheep. Paolo was looking into the pen. "Captain Biddle got them cheaply in trade in San Diego," he said. "Other animal— pigs, young bullocks, and chickens—will be brought on board in Santa Barbara to feed us on the long voyage home to Boston."

Anita looked toward the forward part of the ship where her father was describing Rancho del Mar to Captain Biddle. In the dusk, she noticed a gray shadow move along the opposite side of the fo'c's'le. She walked quietly toward it along the deck. It was Mr. Slope, listening to what Don José was saying. Anita almost bumped into the Yankee when he turned around suddenly. Startled, she jumped back. He glared at her and walked away aft.

What a sneaky thing to do, thought Anita. Why, that means he can understand Spanish. Wonder why he's snooping about.

That night as Don José tucked her in the bunk, she said, "Mr. Slope understands Spanish. He wrote things in his little book while you and the captain were talking at dinner. He followed you and Captain Biddle out on deck. I saw him standing in the shadows listening to you."

Don José's smile disappeared and his face became sober. "He is a very strange man. He makes me uneasy. I'm going to be very careful what I say in front of him. Captain Biddle says he is interested in setting up a business in Santa Barbara."

"He certainly made a lot of notes when you and the captain were talking at dinner about Rancho del Mar and our boundaries."

"Well, don't worry about it. Go to sleep," said Don José as he kissed her goodnight. He turned down the flame in the oil lamp and lay down in his bunk.

For a long time Anita heard him tossing and turning while the spars creaked and the wind whistled in the rigging. She wondered what dark thoughts nibbled at the back of his mind.

RESCUE AT SEA

*A*fter breakfast the next morning, Anita watched the beautiful island of Santa Catalina pass off the port bow. Standing by her side, Captain Biddle described the different sea animals that lived in the islands of the Santa Barbara Channel. "On the western beaches of the islands," he said, "elephant seals live in big colonies on the sand. When we sail past the Channel Islands on the seaward side, we can hear them barking."

"What's that red thing out there, Captain Biddle?" asked Anita. "Is that a kind of sea animal?"

"Where?"

"Off to the right, up ahead."

The captain squinted in the sunlight. Then he hurried inside his cabin and came out with a telescope. He put it to his eye and looked steadily at the red spot bobbing in the sea. "Mr. Starbuck, we have sighted a man in the water, two points off the starboard bow. Boston Billy, climb the mast and see what you can see."

Boston Billy, who had the sharpest eyes on the ship, clambered up the mast. When he reached the skysail spar, he yelled down through cupped hands, "Man in a red shirt floating on a water cask, Captain."

"Bring the ship into the wind and heave to," called out Captain Biddle. "Mr. Starbuck, lower the longboat." The *Pride of Nantucket* came up into the wind and stopped dead in the water.

Mr. Slope hurried over to the Captain. "Why are we stopping? I demand you keep sailing for Santa Barbara. I have important business that won't wait."

Captain Biddle answered through his teeth in his captain-of-the-ship voice. "Mr. Slope, the rules of the sea require that we stand to and rescue a shipwrecked man."

The longboat crew scrambled to their places. The boat swung out on the davits and the sailors carefully lowered it to the sea. The crew rowed smoothly and powerfully through the waves to the bobbing water cask. They pulled a severely sunburned man aboard and rowed back to the brig. Other sailors gently lifted the red-shirted man to the deck.

"Is he dead?" asked Don José.

"Still alive, sir, but in a very bad state," answered Paolo.

"Hmph, more waste of time," complained Mr. Slope.

The man's face and arms were burned a bright red. His eyes were swollen and he couldn't open them. His lips were so blistered that he couldn't speak.

"We found him in time, or rather Anita did," said Captain Biddle. "Paolo, put him in the lee of the cabin, out of the sun and wind. Take off his wet clothes and wrap him in a blanket. He needs liquids after being in the water for so long."

Anita knew what to do. She went to the cook and returned with some olive oil and a bowl of chicken broth. She gently swabbed the blisters on the man's lips with the oil. Spoonful by spoonful, she fed him the warm chicken broth. "Mother always says that chicken broth is good for you when you are sick." The man raised one hand weakly to thank her.

From a box in his cabin Captain Biddle brought out a hollow bamboo reed. Anita placed it in a cup of water so that the man might sip it a little at a time. She sat by him all day and took care of him. To amuse herself she borrowed some paper from Don José's notebook and drew pictures of the latest San Diego styles in fiesta dresses and hair arrangements for María Isabel and Tía Luisa.

Captain Biddle decided that it would be too painful for the man to be lifted down the ladder to the crew's quarters below. The evening air was warm and pleasant, so the sailors made a bed for him among the sailbags and covered him with blankets. The captain ordered the seamen on night watch to check that he was covered and to hold the cup so that he could take small drinks of water.

Mr. Slope resented the efforts of the captain and the crew to help the man. He complained again about wasted time. "Rank incompetence!"

As the *Pride of Nantucket* sailed back to Santa Barbara, the rescued man slowly regained his strength. The skin on his arms peeled off in sheets. At times he burned with fever, other times he shivered with cold.

Late on the fourth day, the man spoke to Anita and Paolo in a croaking voice. Paolo translated, "He says his name is

Abner Prescott from Maine in the United States. He was hunting sea otters in a longboat with two other men when they were overturned by a high wave. The other men were lost, but he was lucky. He grabbed the water cask and stayed afloat. He had been in the water many hours when we found him."

"Tell him that Captain Biddle will bring him to Mission Santa Barbara tomorrow where the *padres* will take care of him until he is well."

"He says this is the last sea voyage he is going to take," said Paolo. "He has been a storekeeper, a farmer, a shoe-maker and a surveyor. From now on he is staying on land. He'll never go otter hunting again."

"Did you say 'surveyor'?" Anita got up from her seat on the coil of rope and walked over to where her father was writing in his notebook. As usual Mr. Slope, like a gray seagull, hovered nearby. "Father, Paolo says the man we rescued is a surveyor. Maybe he could work for you on the ranch."

Don José crossed the deck and talked to the rescued man while Paolo translated from Spanish to English and back again. Don José wrote down the name "Abner Prescott" in his notebook. Then he tore out a blank page and wrote his own name and the address of Rancho Santa Cruz del Mar. He handed the paper to Mr. Prescott who thanked him and put it away carefully in his pocket.

A short time later, Anita saw Mr. Slope sidle over to the otter hunter and start asking him questions. Behind Mr. Slope's back, Paolo put his finger to his lips to signal Abner Prescott not to talk. Mr. Prescott touched his throat and pretended he could not speak.

As the brig sailed past the River Santa Clara, Anita pointed out to Mr. Prescott the smoke from the ranch house. "That's where we live." They saw the white bell tower of Mission San Buenaventura. Anita felt glad because she knew she would be home in a few days. She sat down on the big coil of rope and began mending the ripped cuff on Boston Billy's "shore-going" shirt.

Of course, Mr. Slope noticed. He never missed anything. He disappeared into his cabin and came out carrying his gray silk coat with the ripped seam. He stalked up to Anita and said, "Here, girl, mend this rip in my coat." He held out a small coin to her.

Anita did not understand the English words. She knew Mr. Slope was ordering her to mend his coat, and she felt insulted by his tone.

Don José saw the strange look on Anita's face and came over to her side immediately. He looked at the coat and the coin and said in icy Spanish, "My daughter is not your servant, Mr. Slope. She neither wants nor needs your coin."

Mr. Slope obviously understood what Don José had said. A mean look crossed his gray face. His cheeks turned a dark red.

Paolo spoke up quickly in English. "I'll mend it for you, *señor*. I have gray silk thread in my sea chest below. I'll have to charge you tailor's wages though. That will be three of those coins."

"All right," Mr. Slope growled. He handed over the coat and stamped off to his cabin.

The sky was clear overhead as the *Pride of Nantucket* approached Santa Barbara, but a heavy curtain of fog hung between the ship and the harbor.

"What will Captain Biddle do now?" Anita asked her father.

"Watch, Captain Biddle will take compass bearings on prominent points of land on Santa Cruz Island. He will plot the position of the ship on the chart. From this position he measures the compass course and the distance to Santa Barbara Harbor. See, he's bringing the ship onto the correct course, from the ship's position plotted on the chart."

"He is sailing the ship right into the fog, Father," cried Anita. "How can he see where he's headed?"

"He can't. He's steering the ship by the compass. He knows how far he has to sail the ship to anchor in the harbor. He drops a taffrail log over the stern of the ship and measures how fast he is going."

The fog enveloped them in a blanket of wet gray velvet. Dark shapes loomed out of the mist. Voices from other ships already anchored in the roadstead sounded hollow and muted. Anita felt uneasy.

"The captain watches the time and measures the distance the ship is traveling," said Don José. "He has a man standing far forward ready to throw a lead weight at the end of a line. The seaman twirls the rope over his head like a lariat and throws it into the water. When the lead weight hits the bottom, they can tell by the marks on the line how deep the water is. Listen."

The seaman twirled the line and the lead weight splashed in the water. He called out, "No bottom, Cap'n. Ten fathoms."

"That means the water here is more than sixty feet deep," explained Don José. "When the ship has sailed a proper distance and they judge the depth of the water to be right, less than ten fathoms, they drop the anchor."

"There's Boston Billy up forward blowing the fog horn," said Anita. "Wouldn't Tonio love to be doing that?"

Don José smiled at the thought. "He certainly would. The captain says the ship that is moving blows the horn as it sails along. The ships at anchor ring bells. Listen. Hear the anchor hawser running out? The ship has stopped moving. We are anchored."

When the fog cleared away the next morning, the ship was exactly where Captain Biddle wanted it to be, anchored in forty feet of water off shore from the bell tower of the Mission.

Don José walked over to the railing where Captain Biddle was looking toward shore. "That was a fine piece of seamanship, sir."

Captain Biddle laughed. "Sometimes we are not so lucky. The last time we anchored in the fog, we anchored downwind from a whaler. The crew complained because it smelled so bad. When the whaler set out to sea the next day, our whole crew lined the rail, held their noses and cheered."

After breakfast Anita gathered her things together in her wicker satchel. Filled with the new doll, the packages of seeds and flower cuttings, and the pretty dresses Josefa had given her, it was hard to close. She had to sit on it before the latch would click into place.

Captain Biddle stood at the gangway as Anita and Don José descended the ladder into the bobbing longboat. Mr. Prescott limped shakily over to the rail where he joined Paolo and the rest of the crew. They all waved and called out, "Goodbye, *Adiós*, Anita." "Come back again." Mr. Slope stayed in his cabin, out of sight.

She looked up at her friends, held on tight to the side of the longboat with one hand and waved with the other. She steadied the wicker basket between her feet. The boat crew rowed quickly to shore and then carried Anita and her father to the beach. Don José thanked the sailors courteously and gave them some silver coins from his pocket.

When Don José turned around, Anita was halfway up

the beach to where Lorenzo waited in a carriage. "I saw the *Pride of Nantucket* anchored in the harbor and drove down to meet you. I really missed you, Little Sister," he said. "It's rather dull without you."

Anita laughed. "I'll bet you didn't miss us at all. I think you saw Cecelia every day."

Don José picked up Anita's wicker satchel and hurried after her across the sand. As he lifted the satchel into the carriage, he said, "It's good to see you, Lorenzo. Where are Enrique and Fernando?"

"They rode back to Rancho del Mar four days ago with our horses to tell the family you'd sailed to San Diego." He started up the team, his eyes twinkling with laughter. "You and Anita shared another of her adventures."

"Yes indeed, your sister attracts adventures the way a flower attracts bees. We have much to talk about, my son. Among other things, I plan to hire a man to make an exact survey of our ranch. Stop here by the ship's agent's office. I want to leave an order for a new gun."

Don José disappeared inside the store. Anita leaned back against the cushions on the carriage seat. The sun felt warm on her face. I woke up early and I'm still sleepy, she thought. Galloping up the street, a pair of riders passed close by the carriage. One was Mr. Slope, his long skinny legs almost touching the ground. The other man was short and heavy set. His dark green cloth coat looked familiar. She yawned. Of course, I see it every Sunday at the Mission. It's Señor Valencia, talking to Mr. Slope like an old friend.

Don José returned to the carriage and began to talk to Lorenzo about new plans for the ranch. Her eyelids drooped. I can't tell him now. He'll be annoyed if I interrupt. I'll tell him later. She really intended to tell her father, but she closed her eyes, fell sound asleep and then forgot to remember.

When they reached the de la Guerra house, Don José and Doña Antonia welcomed Anita and her father warmly. Two de la Guerra girls took Anita to a far corner of the patio to show her a special secret. There, on some old wool blankets were not one, but two litters of kittens. Mewing softly, the kittens scampered about and rolled over one another. Their little tails were standing straight up like tiny fish poles.

At dinner that evening, Doña Antonia asked many questions about the Bandinis. Anita described the fiesta, the circus, the *cascarones,* and the new dance called the waltz.

Doña Antonia was fascinated with the idea of a new dance. After dinner she insisted that Anita and her father show everyone how to waltz.

"Querido," begged Doña Antonia, "please order a copy of the new dance music. We can introduce the waltz at our next party."

"The *padres* may not approve," warned her husband.

"Oh, fiddle faddle!" sniffed Doña Antonia. "If the waltz is danced in the Emperor's court in Vienna, we can dance it in Santa Barbara."

Early the following morning Anita, Lorenzo and Don José got into a *carreta.* Tucked around Anita's feet were small packages of seeds and rose cuttings, a basket filled with a mouth-watering, savory lunch to eat on the way, the wicker basket from San Diego, and the three leather bags in which their traveling clothes had been packed.

At the last minute two giggling de la Guerra girls pushed a large basket with a tight cover into Anita's arms. She smiled and carefully balanced it on her lap.

They had just passed the place called *"Sal si puedes"* on Camino Real when Don José turned around suddenly and looked back at Anita. "There it is again. What's that sound?"

Skritch! Skritch! *"Miu, miu, miau!"* The Spanish speaking kittens scratched at the lid from the inside.

"Anita, what do you have in that basket — a cat?"

"Please, Father, it's only two kittens. The de la Guerras had so many. They are for Beatriz. The mice have been getting into the storeroom. Tonio says they hold fiestas on the sacks of flour every night. Please let me keep them. I've already named them. The black one with the white ring around his neck is El Duque de Alba and the lovely yellow cat with the long hair is named La Reina Victoria. Of course, Princess Victoria hasn't been crowned Queen yet, but she soon will be."

Don José glanced at Lorenzo, smiled and shrugged his shoulders. "With such distinguished names, I suppose they should be considered special guests in our house. Don't open that basket. If they jumped out, a red tailed hawk would make a fine dinner of them in fifteen minutes."

All the long way home the *carreta* lurched along the bumpy narrow road. The kittens mewed and scratched to get out of the basket. Don José and Lorenzo discussed new plans for Rancho del Mar. Anita sat quietly thinking of all the exciting things that had happened to her in the past two weeks. She felt older somehow. She remembered the whale. That's a secret that I want to keep just for myself.

It was growing dark as the team of oxen crossed the dry bed of the Ventura River and plodded along Camino Real to the Mission. "Stop here for a moment, Lorenzo," said Don José. "I want to speak to the *padre*." He went inside the Mission garden and in a few words told the *padre* the news from Monterey about the governor's proclamations. The *padre* looked troubled and thoughtful as he came outside with Don José. Then he told two Indians from the Mission to ride ahead of the *carreta*. Each held a blazing torch to light the way on the last five miles of the journey. Home to Rancho del Mar, thought Anita.

From the second floor of the ranch house the family saw the lighted torches coming along the road. Tonio and the twins mounted their horses and galloped off to greet the travelers.

As they drove through the courtyard gate, everyone came out to welcome them home. Don José called Tomás aside and told him to make sure that the Chumash Indian riders from the Mission had food to eat and a place to spend the night.

Anita and Lorenzo entered the brightly lit *sala*. Everybody was talking and asking questions all at once.

"*Ay, Chihuahua,* Anita! What have you done to your hair? You look older."

"It's the latest fashion."

"Who fixed your hair that new way?" asked Tía Luisa. "I like it."

"Doña Refugio," answered Anita. "I like it too. It's called a French braid."

The noise stopped only when Don José came into the *sala*, kissed his wife, raised his hands up high and said, "Home at last."

Anita still held the basket with a tight grip. The two kittens were frantic from the noise and pushed on the lid of their wicker prison. She lifted the cover. El Duque de Alba leaped out, scampered across the floor, and hid under Tía Luisa's chair. He peered suspiciously from under her long skirts while Anita handed La Reina Victoria to Beatriz.

"They will keep the mice out of the storeroom, Beatriz," said Anita. "They really need some milk now as they haven't eaten all day."

"We'll take care of that right away," said Beatriz. Off she went to the kitchen with La Reina Victoria for a saucer of milk.

María Isabel followed her and returned to the *sala* with another saucer of milk. "He's so cute." She put the milk down on the floor by El Duque and coaxed him to try it. His hunger and thirst were greater than his fear of a new place. He lapped up all the milk, purred and rubbed against Tía Luisa's skirt. With his little tail standing straight up like a fish pole, he looked happy and contented.

"I'll take him to the kitchen. The kittens can stay there in their basket," said Anita. She returned in a few minutes saying, "They are both sound asleep."

"You should be, too," said Don José. "You woke early this morning and have been bumping along the road all day."

"But aren't we going to hear what happened on the trip?" protested María Isabel.

"There will be plenty of time tomorrow to tell us everything," said Doña Francisca. "Goodnight, dear."

"Goodnight, Mother," yawned Anita. "Goodnight everyone." Five minutes later she was tucked in her own bed, her doll Marina on the pillow. She heard the horned owls hoot to each other in the trees outside her window. One hoot for the male, two hoots for the female. "Gabby, like all women," Tonio had said. Her last thought before sliding off to sleep was, it's good to be home again.

MR. O'LEARY

The family gathered in the *sala* for early morning chocolate. Later they would eat a full breakfast after Don José made his tour of inspection and gave the day's orders to the *vaqueros*.

"A rider from Mission San Fernando told Tomás this morning that a convict has escaped from San Gabriel. He is supposed to be moving north toward Santa Barbara. I'm worried about leaving you ladies alone in the ranch house. The boys and I have to ride to the eastern end of the ranch to round up a herd of wild horses."

"Don't worry about us, José," said Doña Francisca as she handed him a cup of chocolate. "Pedro and Beatriz will be here. We won't be entirely alone. Ranch business must not come to a full stop because of a mere rumor. That does not mean that we should not be alert."

Don José's green eyes smiled at his wife over the rim of his chocolate cup, but his voice took on a serious note. "The *aventada* is very important to us. We need more range mounts for the next roundup. Each extra *vaquero* we hire requires a string of four or five spare horses to part out the cattle."

Anita placed a basket of warm tortillas wrapped in a white cloth by his elbow. "Beatriz says the soldiers took away all Padre Ordaz' horses except one. They helped themselves to blankets and food and told him to send the bill to the governor. Couldn't we give him an extra horse or two?"

Don José frowned. "Yes, we could. It is a bad situation all around and not all the fault of the soldiers. The Mexican government has not paid them in months. Their boots are worn out, their clothes in rags. Morale is poor. There is not a complete uniform among the six men in the *cuartel*. The same thing has happened all over California."

"We can not expect the soldiers to come and guard us," Tía Luisa said. "Leave your pistols with me. We can take care of ourselves."

"I still have my father's pistol. He taught me how to shoot." Doña Francisca looked calmly at her husband. "I will use it if I have to."

"I will leave the old Spanish miquelet musket with Pedro. Anita, you and María Isabel should stay close to the ranch house until we return. No riding off by yourselves, even to the beach."

Anita felt disappointed. She loved to ride through the surf, but she would not disobey her father. It didn't help at all when Tonio whispered in her ear and said, "You'll have to stay home, Little Sister, and leave the work to us men." He grinned at her as he chewed on a tortilla.

" 'Us men'! What do you mean 'us men'? You're only thirteen." She glared at him and tossed her head. She would have liked to go along and watch the *aventada* from a distance, but she had no desire to take part in the dusty, dirty, tiring work of separating out the horses.

After the male members of the family left, Doña Francisca held a meeting in the *sala*. "We will take turns keeping lookout on the balcony all day. Pedro will stand guard in the courtyard. If someone does come in, you will go into the storeroom, Anita; María Isabel will hide in the cornfield. Be quiet as mice. The rest of us will handle the situation."

Anita paced the balcony in the late afternoon, watching both directions along Camino Real. El Duque and La Reina Victoria sat on the railing, their tails twitching nervously.

As she stared toward the sea, a moving black speck on the road caught her eye. A jolt of fear hit her deep inside. She eyed the approaching speck. It took on the appearance of a man striding along the road. He wore a straw hat, a ragged coat and torn pants. He looked very dirty.

She ran downstairs and gasped, "Mother, someone is coming. He looks like a tramp."

Doña Francisca put aside her sewing and took charge like the *comandante's* daughter she was. They loaded the pistols and the musket. Each person went to his assigned station.

Anita entered the storeroom at the corner of the house. How odd, she thought, he's coming from the west, not the east. He doesn't walk like a *vaquero* either. She climbed up on an old chest, brushed away the cobwebs and peered through a tiny window set high in the adobe wall. She had to know what was going to happen. An eerie stillness filled the deserted courtyard. Her heart thumped in her chest. She watched and waited.

Light footsteps approached along the path outside the wall. A young man in torn and dirty clothes, wearing a neat straw Panama hat and carrying a small bag slung over his shoulder, entered the courtyard with a confident stride. He was halfway across the courtyard when Pedro said sharply, "Hands up!" The grim-faced young *vaquero* held the old, well-oiled Spanish musket in firing position. The stranger dropped his bag and slowly raised his hands in the air.

Tía Luisa's angry voice rang out from the balcony, "We have already been robbed once, Señor Bandido. This time we are ready. Believe me, I won't hesitate to shoot." The two pistols clicked as she cocked them.

From the *sala* came Doña Francisca, waving a pistol, a determined look on her gentle face. Close behind her marched brave Beatriz, brandishing her sharp skinning knife.

"Holy Saint Patrick," said the stranger.

Anita jumped down from the chest in the storeroom and hurried to the courtyard, her dark curls bobbing on her shoulders. "It's Mr. O'Leary! How nice to see you again. Welcome to Rancho del Del Mar."

"In truth, I am indeed very glad to see you, Anita," said Mr. O'Leary his hands still raised in the air.

"Mr. O'Leary?" cried Doña Francisca. "I am so sorry. Please lower your hands. Pedro, it's all right. Mr. O'Leary is a friend who will be staying with us."

Up on the balcony Tía Luisa laughed out loud. "We saw you coming a long way off. We thought you were an outlaw." She went inside, carefully uncocked the pistols and emptied out the powder and balls. She put away the pistols in their case and stepped gracefully down the balcony stairs to greet the new tutor.

Anita presented Mr. O'Leary to Doña Francisca. She held out her hand and he bent over it, his lips just above, but not touching her fingers. He had learned that custom in Paris and it had never failed to charm married ladies.

Anita introduced Tía Luisa as Señora del Valle. Tía Luisa smiled at Mr. O'Leary as he bent over her hand. She had not had her hand kissed like that since the time she had met a French count long ago in Mexico City.

Curious about Tía Luisa's laughter and the lack of commotion in the courtyard, María Isabel left the cornfield and cautiously walked around the corner of the ranch house.

"This is my sister, María Isabel," said Anita, and to her sister, "This is Mr. O'Leary."

María Isabel was so surprised that she forgot to flirt.

Because gentlemen do not kiss the hands of unmarried young ladies, Mr. O'Leary made a graceful bow to María Isabel instead.

"I am happy to meet you, *señor*," she said. He looked at her as if she were the most beautiful girl he had seen in California.

"Come into the *sala*," said Doña Francisca. "We'll have some *refresco*."

"*Señora*, my clothes are so muddy that I wouldn't think of entering your *sala* until I change them," said Mr. O'Leary.

"Well, in that case, let us all sit out here on the porch. We can drink some *refresco* here in the shade while Beatriz heats some water for your bath. You can tell us what happened to you."

"I left early this morning from Carpinteria and my horse went lame before I reached the Mission. Padre Ordaz was visiting a sick person, but a kind Indian woman at the Mission gave me lunch and directions to Rancho del Mar. She promised to take care of the horse for me. I set off down the road and was enjoying a fine walk in the bracing air when I met a large bull that chased me off the road. I jumped into the *chaparral,* tore my clothes, just missed bumping into a thorny cactus, and fell into the mud before I could get back on the road again."

"I'll tell Pedro about that stray bull. He'll round him up," said Anita. "It's not safe to go on foot along Camino Real."

While they were talking, María Isabel brought out a tray of glasses filled with Doña Francisca's special *refresco.* Mr. O'Leary sipped it with appreciation. "I haven't tasted *refresco* like this since I was in Seville."

"You must tell us about your travels this evening at dinner," said Doña Francisca. "José and the boys will be home this evening."

"Your bath is ready, *señor*," Beatriz announced.

"Amelia will show you to your room, Mr. O'Leary. If you put out your muddy riding clothes and boots, the maids will clean them for you," said Doña Francisca.

"Thank you very much," he replied.

Mr. O'Leary picked up his bag and followed Amelia to his room. Then he poured out the pitchers of hot and cold water into the big copper tub that the maids had carried upstairs. After bathing he took a razor from his bag and shaved himself carefully in a small mirror. By the time he had changed into clean clothes and soft slippers, he heard the clatter of horses below and Don José's voice calling out, "Francisca, we're home. Where are you?"

Mr. O'Leary folded his muddy clothes in a neat pile and went downstairs to meet his employer. The five horsemen dismounting by the porch were covered with dust and dirt. Doña Francisca sent them all off to the wash house where soap, hot water, towels and clean clothes were waiting.

Tonio strutted past Anita, his face covered with dirt and perspiration. "Too bad girls can't go to the *aventada*, Anita. It was fun."

"Don't forget to wash behind your ears," whispered Anita as he walked away. "Sometimes he makes me so mad," she said to Mr. O'Leary. "He never lets me forget that he's a boy and I'm a girl. He still treats me like a baby sister."

"How many horses did you round up today, Father?" called María Isabel from the porch.

"We captured twenty-five. They are in a box canyon a few miles from here. We put a temporary fence across the opening to keep them in." Don José greeted Mr. O'Leary warmly and followed his sons to the wash house.

Mr. O'Leary watched Don José and his four sons as they walked away. All were as lean as whips and taller than most Californians he had met.

That evening at the dinner table the Lorenzanas became acquainted with the new member of the household. They found him a pleasant talker who did not take over the conversation, but kept them laughing with stories about his student days in Dublin. Anita noted that the new tutor asked good questions about life on the rancho.

"Mr. O'Leary, have some of these special peppers," offered Enrique, passing the bowl down the table.

"They're so good," said his twin, Fernando, taking one and placing it on his plate.

María Isabel took the bowl from him and said sweetly to her brother, "Perhaps Mr. O'Leary would like to try Mother's special olives instead." She passed the olives to the new tutor while Anita looked reproachfully at the twins and placed the chile peppers out of Mr. O'Leary's reach.

Mr. O'Leary accepted the olives and thanked María Isabel with a smile. He knows about green *chiles*, Anita remembered. He told me how Felix Bandini had played that practical joke on him in San Diego. Those little innocent looking green *chiles* had set his tongue on fire, paralyzed his tonsils, and when he gulped down some cold water, he was sure that steam was coming out of his ears. He'll have to watch his step with the twins.

"These olives are delicious, Doña Francisca, and I do believe, Beatriz is the best cook in California," said Mr. O'Leary.

Beatriz overheard him as she brought in another platter of tender seared steak. From then on, as far as she was concerned, Mr. O'Leary could do no wrong.

Mr. O'Leary turned to Don José, "How do you round up twenty-five wild horses, *señor*?"

"We call it *aventada*. Our wild horses are small, but tough and wiry, and very fast. With a saddle, they make good horses for certain kinds of ranch work."

"First we have to find the wild horses," said Lorenzo with a laugh. "That's not as easy as you might think."

"After we find them," said Don José, "I station *vaqueros* every two miles or so across the valley. "At a signal two *vaqueros* set off after the wild horses as fast as their mounts will carry them, heading the wild ones toward the waiting *vaqueros*. The stallion leader suddenly appears out of the band of horses which quickly huddle together and stand very still. Their nostrils are open wide and their heads and tails are erect. The stallion turns and circles his band. Then they all start galloping over the valley floor."

Enrique spoke up, "It's a wild ride because the ground

is full of gopher holes. If your mount steps in one, he may trip and throw you. The wild horses get more and more confused as we race after them, especially when Fernando and the *vaqueros* spring up on either side and shout to make them run faster. Even when the ground is covered with grass, a huge cloud of dust covers everything. You can't hear anything but the thunder of hoofs."

"We keep this up for two or three hours," Fernando added. "The *vaqueros* manage to get into the center of the flying herd. When the dust finally clears, you can see the young horses here and there over the valley floor. Tonio and the *vaqueros* have lassoed them during the chase and tied their forelegs to keep them from escaping. That's how we were able to capture twenty-five horses today."

"Your mounts have to be stronger and faster than the wild horses."

"Our mounts are fed on grain," answered Don José. "The wild horses eat only grass. It's the grain that makes the difference."

"We'll start breaking some of the four-year-olds to the saddle tomorrow," said Enrique. "Would you like to come and watch us?"

"Tomás will take charge of that, Enrique. Tomorrow morning everyone will start English and mathematics lessons here in the *sala*," said his father.

EL CID

*A*fter breakfast the following morning, Mr. O'Leary began tutoring his six pupils. Actually there was a seventh. Tía Luisa came into the *sala* and sat in the chair by the window mending the tears in Mr. O'Leary's tweed coat. Anita noticed her aunt was following the English lesson closely.

Everyone did well except the twins. All they can think about is breaking those wild horses, said Anita to herself. How they hate to be cooped up in the house.

As the days went by, Mr. O'Leary's students settled into a routine of class in the morning and ranch duties in the afternoon. Lorenzo would sit in a quiet corner and read the history of ancient Rome. Anita and Tonio would work on arithmetic problems. Everyone except Anita was surprised when María Isabel turned out to have a natural gift for geometry. Enrique and Fernando were annoyed because she always finished the problems before they did.

Mr. O'Leary's trunks arrived by cart from Santa Barbara. Padre Ordaz lent some books from the small Mission library and showed a lively interest in Lorenzo's study of ancient Rome. From time to time the *padre* would send English and American newspapers to Rancho del Mar. Although the tattered and worn copies were often two years old, Mr. O'Leary devoured them column by column the way Tonio ate through a plateful of cookies. The young Lorenzanas learned to read English from the newspapers.

One bright sunny morning there was one interruption after another. Just as Anita settled down to her multiplication problems, El Duque de Alba stalked proudly into the room and deposited a dead mouse at Tía Luisa's feet. Then he sat down in front of her and waited to be praised. The twins looked up and grinned. Anita and María Isabel giggled.

"Tonio, please take that awful thing outside," begged Tía Luisa. She pulled her skirts away from the dead offering.

Tonio left his arithmetic problems and picked up the mouse by its tail. He rewarded El Duque with a gentle scratch behind his ear and took the mouse outside.

When everyone had settled down quietly to work again, a loud shout from the corral indicated a *vaquero* had been bucked off a wild horse he was trying to break. Immediately everybody looked up. The twins rushed over to the doorway to see what had happened. "He's not hurt," Enrique called over his shoulder to his brothers and sisters. Mr. O'Leary was exasperated with the interruptions, but he patiently brought his students back to their work.

Then the cheery voice of Padre Ordaz was heard greeting Don José and Doña Francisca. His thin figure in its gray robe appeared in the doorway. He saw the students busy working and came in silently on sandaled feet. He placed a pile of books and newspapers on a table, nodded to Mr. O'Leary, and padded out of the room. The students looked curiously at the pile of books and newspapers.

Mr. O'Leary surrendered. "That's enough work for this morning, everyone. Tomorrow you can finish the mathematics test," he said to the twins. "I think I'll go for a ride."

The twins looked at one another. They could read each other's thoughts at a glance. "We'll have a horse saddled for you," said Enrique quickly. He and Fernando strode off to the corral.

They're up to something, Anita thought as she put away her work.

Mr. O'Leary went to his room and came out wearing a pair of low-heeled, high-topped riding boots that rose to his knees. He wore no spurs. Anita walked down to the corral where Padre Ordaz, Don José, and the twins waited to see him off. She was shocked to see the *vaquero* leading out a saddled and bridled El Cid from the corral. El Cid was a horse that wanted his own way. He liked best to leap over walls and throw off unsuspecting riders.

Anita noticed Enrique and Fernando were wearing the guileless look of altar boy innocence they always wore when playing a practical joke. They had not been doing well on Mr. O'Leary's mathematics test. Now the students would test their tutor.

If Mr. O'Leary noticed the twins' efforts to keep straight faces, he gave no sign. "What a magnificent horse," he said admiringly.

Anita started to say something, but the *padre* winked at her and put his finger to his lips. She glanced at Tomás and saw a rare smile on his tanned face. She knew Tomás liked

Mr. O'Leary, and stopped worrying. I'll wait and see what happens, she thought.

Mr. O'Leary walked over to El Cid and looked him straight in the eyes. Then he said something in a low voice to the horse who pricked up his ears and moved restlessly. The tutor patted El Cid's neck and ran his hand along the horse's side and flank. He walked all the way around him speaking softly in a strange language. Next Mr. O'Leary did an odd thing; he breathed into El Cid's nostrils. Then he moved around to the left side, mounted quickly and turned El Cid toward the ocean.

Enrique slapped Fernando on the back and laughed. "Watch. El Cid's going to go over that wall. Mr. O'Leary will be *patas arriba* in a minute."

El Cid approached the wall at a gallop, quite sure that the man on his back would not be there long. The horse leaped confidently over the wall, but Mr. O'Leary kept his seat and was not thrown off.

"I didn't see any daylight between him and the saddle," remarked Don José. "It seems Don Eduardo has jumped a few walls before that one."

"Oh, didn't you know?" said the *padre* matter of factly. "Don Eduardo grew up on a farm in Ireland where his father raised jumping horses for English fox hunters."

Anita laughed at the expressions on the twins' faces. The joke was on them. "He rides El Cid better than we can," Fernando admitted.

An hour later Mr. O'Leary rode back on a docile El Cid. Anita asked, "What were those words you were saying to El Cid before you got up in the saddle?"

"I spoke to him in Gaelic," said Mr. O'Leary.

"What did you say?"

"I told him that if he did what I knew he was planning

to do, I would make a cart horse out of him in five minutes."

"Gaelic, eh? And he understood you?"

"Oh, yes, he's a very smart horse indeed," said Mr. O'Leary. "Of course, I used a little blarney. Maybe that helped."

"What's blarney?"

Mr. O'Leary smiled. "It's Irish sweet talk."

"Oh, I know," said Anita. "That's how Enrique answers Mother when she begs him to stop riding those wild horses. There's one thing I don't understand. Why did you breathe into El Cid's nose?"

"That's a trick I learned from an Irish gypsy," said Mr. O'Leary.

The next afternoon, after barely passing his mathematics test, Enrique made up his mind to ride El Cid. "If Mr. O'Leary can ride him over the wall, so can I," he boasted to Fernando and Anita. He had a *vaquero* saddle El Cid. Enrique walked confidently over to the horse, and swung up into the saddle. However, Enrique could not speak Gaelic. El Cid bucked mightily and tossed Enrique *patas arriba* in the soft smelly earth of the corral. Except for his wounded pride, Enrique was unhurt.

El Cid tossed his head and trotted disdainfully to the other side of the corral where Mr. O'Leary was looking over the fence. El Cid nickered. Mr. O'Leary reached over, patted his neck, and spoke softly in Gaelic. El Cid had become a one-man horse.

10

QUE SERÁ, SERÁ

*A*nita worried about Enrique. Doña Francisca worried about him, too. Enrique had always wanted to do everything better than his twin. He wanted to run faster, climb higher, ride wilder horses and rope more grizzlies than anyone else. Fernando did all these things well, but he was the cautious twin. Enrique liked to find out how close he could come to danger without being hurt. When they were small boys, Enrique used to walk along the river bank as close to the quicksand as he could without falling in. Fernando would walk right behind him, but with a difference. Fernando had his lariat looped around his waist with the other end securely tied to the pommel of his horse's saddle.

"Chicken," Enrique would say.

"Not chicken. If you fall in, I have to be ready to pull you out."

Not long after Mr. O'Leary had tamed El Cid, the *vaqueros* captured a beautiful black stallion and brought him back to the ranch. They called him El Diablo because he was mean through and through. He bit and fought other horses at every opportunity. Even when tied to the corral fence, he would kick savagely at anything that came near. One *vaquero* tried to ride him, was bucked off, and fell inside the corral. El Diablo charged and tried to stamp him with his forefeet. Only quick rope work by Tomás and Pedro saved the man's life. It would take more than Irish blarney to tame El Diablo.

"I have never liked that horse," said Don José. "I don't trust him. He has the makings of a mankiller. It's not good to have him around the other horses."

"Tomás says he's fit only for condor meat," replied Fernando.

Don José left the corral and walked back to the house. Enrique saw his father disappear through the doorway of his office. "I can break El Diablo," he said.

"Don't waste your time on him." Anita was concerned about her headstrong brother. "Break that pretty Appaloosa for me, the one with the snowflake marks on his hindquarters."

"No." Enrique's face had a stubborn look. "I'm going to break El Diablo."

Doña Francisca always stayed away from the corral and its strong animal smells. Now she hurried over to the corral fence and stood alongside Anita. "Enrique, you take too many chances. I'm afraid you will be hurt some day riding those wild horses."

"Oh, Mother, don't worry so much. I can break anything on four legs," he boasted. "Anyway, *que será, será.*"

141

Fernando, the cautious twin, knew he could not talk Enrique out of riding El Diablo. He frowned in disapproval and said, "He's a mean one. I don't think it's worth the trouble to break him. Even if you do break him, what we'll have is a mean, unreliable work horse."

Practical thinking and common sense had no effect on Enrique. In the contest of wills between Enrique and El Diablo, Enrique had made up his mind. He would be the winner.

"Enrique, don't do it," begged his mother. "There are plenty of other wild horses you can break."

"No, I want to break this one," he said stubbornly. He shrugged his shoulders and smiled at her. *"Que será, será."*

A mounted *vaquero* led the blindfolded and saddled El Diablo into the chute. Tomás sat up on the top rail of the corral fence with his lariat in his hands. He motioned to Pedro, who was sitting on the opposite side of the corral to have his lariat ready, too.

As Enrique jumped into the saddle, the mounted *vaquero* pulled off the blindfold and moved his horse quickly out of the way. El Diablo burst out of the chute. He shivered, stamped his feet, lowered his head and bucked. Enrique stayed in the saddle, but his right stirrup was twisted. El Diablo's red and angry eyes bulged with hate. He suddenly gave a lurch and threw the force of his massive body against the corral fence. Enrique's foot caught in the stirrup. He could not get his right leg out of the way in time. He gave one anguished cry of pain as his leg bone cracked against the corral post. El Diablo bucked again and Enrique fell into the mud and horse droppings. Fernando rushed over to his brother as El Diablo snorted triumphantly and galloped to the other side of the corral.

With a shrill whinny he wheeled around to charge his enemy.

Tomás threw his lasso around El Diablo's neck and snubbed the rope around a post. Pedro lassoed a foreleg and the mounted *vaquero* roped a hindleg. El Diablo lay helpless on the ground, screaming in fury.

Doña Francisca shrieked. "José, come quickly."

Don José rushed from his office. His face turned white when he saw his son's leg twisted. He and Fernando carried Enrique inside and laid him on a bed. Anita followed them in a daze. She felt as if she were living a bad dream. Enrique's mouth was set in a straight line. Drops of sweat stood out on his forehead. Then he fainted from the pain.

They cut off his boot and cut away his trouser leg. Their worst fear was realized. The broken leg bone had pierced the skin leaving it open to infection from the dirt in the corral. Don José and Doña Francisca looked at each other. The unspoken words "blood poisoning" flashed through Anita's mind. Doña Francisca's eyes filled with tears. She stifled a sob and then regained her composure. She called for water and a clean towel and began to clean the wound as best she could.

Don José walked to his gun rack, lifted out a musket, and took some cartridges and lead balls from a drawer in his desk. He picked up the powder horn and went outside. Calling Tomás, he handed him the gun, powder, paper cartridges, and lead balls. "You and Pedro take that horse to Conejo Canyon and destroy him." Don José was grim when he came back to the porch. His other children clustered around him anxiously.

"How is Enrique, Father?" asked Fernando.

"Is there anything we can do?" Lorenzo's voice cracked.

"He is very badly hurt and in danger of blood poisoning. He is in great pain. Ride to the Mission and ask the *padre* for some laudanum."

The nearest doctor lived in Monterey, hundreds of miles to the north. Blood poisoning meant a slow painful death; only laudanum could ease the pain.

An hour later Lorenzo and Fernando returned with the *padre*. He looked at the open wound and gave Enrique the last rites of the Church. Then he brought the family outside and said in a soft voice, "I am very sorry, but you must accept the truth. The leg is very bad. The only thing you can do is give him laudanum."

Don José wrapped his arms around Doña Francisca. She cried into his shoulder. Then she wiped away her tears and hid her sorrow behind a calm face.

As the days dragged by, Tía Luisa retreated to her room and prayed for a miracle. María Isabel quietly took over the management of the daily household routine. Anita helped where she could. Don José and his sons threw themselves into hard physical activity, roping horses, and staking cattle hides out to dry under the hot sun. They stayed away from the silent ranch house as much as possible.

Young people from neighboring ranchos rode many miles to give comfort to the family. Enrique was a popular young man who had many friends. Even Chief Santiago came to help.

Anita led the stately Chumash chief to the porch. Her broken-hearted mother sat outside the room where Enrique lay so quiet and still. Doña Francisca rose and brought the chief to her son's bedside. Then she left and sat down wearily on the bench alongside Anita.

Don José left his office and walked over to his wife. Anita was shocked to hear his hoarse and angry whisper.

"Francisca, are you crazy? Letting him come into Enrique's room to chant and wave feathers and put herbs on that wound."

"I don't care. I'd permit anyone to see Enrique if it would help," she said with tears in her eyes. "Besides, the *padre* says he is a healer."

Chief Santiago looked at the open wound and saw how the blood poisoning had spread. His face was sad as he shook his head knowing his herbs would do no good. Doña Francisca thanked him for trying to help and the dignified chief went quietly away.

In the two weeks that followed Enrique steadily grew worse. The laudanum killed the pain, but he did not recognize anyone. One evening Anita entered the sick room to take her turn watching Enrique. Don José sat in a chair by the bed holding his son's hand. Tears were coursing down his cheeks. Anita had never seen her father cry. She slipped her arm around his shoulders to comfort him.

His voice cracking with emotion, Don José whispered, "What a *Gran Capitán* he would have been in Old Spain. He was born three hundred years too late." Then he wiped away his tears and quietly left the room.

Later that same evening, as Anita put a cold cloth on his forehead, Enrique woke up and tried to speak. She bent her head down close to his face and heard him say, *"Que será, será, Mamá. Que será, será."* He dropped into a deep sleep. A few hours later his spirit slipped away in the quiet darkness of the night.

They laid Enrique to rest in the cemetery of Mission Santa Barbara alongside his grandfather, Don Francisco Toral. The de la Guerras and the Carrillos invited the family to eat a light *merienda* before returning to Rancho del Mar. In a low voice, Don José thanked them and asked to be excused. The slow *carreta* had to pass that narrow place on the coast road before the surf rolled in with the high tide.

When the Lorenzanas made ready to leave, Padre Durán handed them a large woven basket filled with *tortillas* and cheese and bottles of orange juice. "Thank you, *Padre*," said Doña Francisca in her quiet way. "You are most kind."

The day had turned dreary with an overcast sky. A light rain began to fall. The grieving family rode along Camino Real, each one thinking private thoughts. Tía Luisa remembered her beloved Fernando. Mr. O'Leary thought of his own lost love and clasped Anita's hand to comfort her. The long hours passed slowly. Finally they arrived at the ranch house to be met by all the house maids and the *vaqueros*.

"Remember, *querida*," said Don José gently as he helped Doña Francisca down from the cart, "life goes on."

At that moment the threatening dark clouds over the ocean parted. The western sun burst through, shining brightly across the valley. A brilliant rainbow appeared. It stretched from Topa Topa to the mountain at Mugu.

"*Que será, será*, Enrique," said Anita softly, her cheeks wet with tears. "*Que será, será.*"

11

SEBASTIÁN AND MOISÉS

Don José walked his spirited black horse through the gateway. He dismounted and threw the reins to a waiting *vaquero*. The silver spurs jingled as he strode across the courtyard to the shade of the ranch house porch. Passing by the *olla* hanging near the door, he poured himself a drink of cool water and drank it slowly. There was a sad and thoughtful look on his handsome face.

"José," said Doña Francisca coming out from the *sala* with Anita, "you're back early. How is Padre Ordaz? Is there any interesting news?" She saw the expression on his face. "What's the matter? Why are you so troubled?"

Her husband put his arm around her shoulders and said gently, "the *padre* told me that Chief Santiago and his wife, Catarina, died last week of the fever and coughing sickness. There was no medicine to save them."

"Oh, no," she whispered. "He was here just a month ago when—" Her face clouded over. "When he came to see Enrique."

"How are Moisés and Sebastián?" Anita's anxious eyes searched her father's face. "They are all right, aren't they?"

"The *padre* did not know," answered Don José. "He told me the Chumash on that *ranchería* are starving. Some have killed their own goats for food. Others have taken cattle from the herds nearby. The *dueño* of Rancho del Agua Dulce is very angry about that. His head *vaquero* has even whipped some of the Chumash."

"The wild cattle on that ranch belonged to the Indians by decree of the King of Spain since the Mission was founded in 1782. That was long before the Mexican government took over the Mission lands," said Doña Francisca, her eyes flashing in anger.

"The whole situation is unjust," replied Don José. "I am extremely concerned about Moisés and Sebastián. If someone kills their goat for food, there will be no milk for Moisés."

"You must go and bring them back to Rancho del Mar. Take the boys and Anita too. She speaks a little Chumash."

"Please let me go with you, Father. I'm worried about him, too."

Don José raised his eyebrows. "I didn't know you spoke any Chumash. Well then, of course you may come along with us tomorrow."

Early the following morning, Don José, Anita, Tonio, Fernando and Lorenzo mounted their horses and took the coast trail north. They rode past San Buenaventura Mission and turned to the right up the Ventura River valley toward the Chumash village of Auhai. There was no laughing, no singing as they followed the valley trail. Each was concerned about what they would find at the Chumash village. They left the cool sea air behind them and made their way through the warm sunshine toward the high mountains. The brown hills unfolded before them.

After riding some distance, Don José suddenly raised his hand and said, "Stop, everyone." They reined in their horses and looked up along the trail.

"What is it?" asked Anita who was last in line.

"There's a group of *vaqueros* up ahead," answered her father. "They seem to be gathering in a circle and looking down at something. Let's ride past them quickly and go on about our business."

When the Lorenzanas came up to the group, they saw El Malo, Rafael Santos, and four *vaqueros* from Rancho del Agua Dulce. Some distance away Anita saw a rider dressed in gray, almost hidden from sight in the deep shadows of the pine trees. It's Mr. Slope, Anita thought. What is he doing at Rancho del Agua Dulce?

She saw that one *vaquero* had thrown his rope around an Indian and had pulled him to the ground. In his arms the Indian held a baby wrapped in a white blanket. Although the rope had forced him to his knees in the dust, the Indian did not drop the baby.

El Malo snapped his whip and said, "I'll teach you not to steal our cattle."

"It's Moisés!" Anita cried out. Before El Malo could raise his whip again, Anita kicked Chocolate and charged forward. In a flurry of dust she pulled Chocolate up short in front of El Malo, shook her finger in his face and said angrily, "You leave my godchild alone! You mean, miserable, wretched man!"

El Malo's mouth fell open. No one had ever dared to

speak to him like that. It was bad enough to face down the grim looking Don José and his three sons, but this hot tempered unpredictable girl shaking her finger two inches from his nose was something else. He backed his horse a few feet. Sebastián, weak from hunger and thirst, struggled up painfully from his knees, still holding his baby son. Rafael Santos sneered at him from a safe distance. Anita glared at Rafael. Then she heard her father's voice.

"Anita," ordered her father, "come back here at once. I'll attend to this." Don José's face was white with controlled anger. He said in icy tones, *"Caporal,* this is my godson. If you ever try to harm him or his father, you will have to answer to me. Do you understand? Take that rope off!"

El Malo spoke in a surly voice, "These Chumash steal the *dueño's* cattle. Thieves have to be taught a lesson." He motioned the *vaquero* to take the rope off Sebastián.

For a moment there was absolute silence. Don José's jaw set and he controlled himself with difficulty. His voice cut through the air like a knife. "The Chumash have always been told by the *padres* that these cattle belong to them by decree of the King of Spain. Your *dueño* is from Mexico and does not know our customs. In California a hungry man may kill a steer provided he leaves the hide and tallow for the *ranchero*. There are thousands of cattle on Rancho del Agua Dulce. If your *dueño* cannot afford to give a few scrawny cows to the starving Chumash, have him speak to me. I'll give him a cow for every one they take," Disgusted and angry, Don José turned away. He fought to keep himself under control. "Fernando, take Moisés and hand him to Anita. Lorenzo, help Sebastián up on the extra horse."

Anita stretched out her arms to hold Moisés. He was too

weak to open his eyes. "Oh, Moisés," she said with tears rolling down her cheeks, "what has happened to you?"

Sebastián would have fallen, but Lorenzo steadied him and helped him mount the horse. Fernando took a bottle from his saddlebag and gave him a drink of water. Sebastián grasped the saddlehorn and slumped over, too far gone to guide the horse. Lorenzo and Fernando moved their horses alongside and held him in the saddle.

"Father, let's go back to the Mission right away." Anita's voice broke with emotion. "We can get food there for Moisés and Sebastián."

"Let's go," responded Don José. Without a backward glance at El Malo, the *ranchero* and his sons turned their horses around and headed down the valley toward the sea. Don José rode in front, followed by Lorenzo and Fernando holding Sebastián upright in the saddle.

Last in line Anita looked with disgust at El Malo. His deep set eyes glinted with malice as he snapped his whip around the trunk of a small tree. Anita heard him mutter something about "high and mighty *gente de razón*," He snapped his whip again. "Don José looks down his nose at me as if I were a bug on a pin."

Rafael Santos pushed his horse alongside El Malo's. "Just wait," he said. "My uncle has a plan. He and Señor Slope will work things out. Before long Don José won't be so high and mighty."

Samuel Slope's mouth twisted into a thin crooked smile. "We have several plans," Anita heard him boast in Spanish.

Contemptible creeps, thought Anita. I'll tell Father what they said. Holding Moisés in her arms, she turned her back on them, fell into place alongside Tonio, and rode away.

At the Mission the kindly cook bustled about, filling

bowls of beef broth for everyone. Tonio fed Sebastián slowly, spoonful by spoonful. Anita held up the baby's little head and fed him sips of broth from her bowl.

Sebastián began to revive and asked for more soup. This time he fed himself. All the while he watched Moisés. The *padre* talked to the young father in Chumash, and Sebastián answered in a low voice.

"Only a few families are left in their *rancheria*," said the *padre* to Don José. "I have advised him not to return there, but to take Moisés and go with you to Rancho del Mar."

"As the baby's godfather, it is my duty to look out for him. We will take good care of Sebastián and Moisés."

"Sebastián is a well trained *vaquero*," remarked the *padre*. "There is not much about horses, cattle and sheep that he doesn't know. When he has recovered, you would do well to have him work for you."

"We can always use a good worker on the ranch. Moisés and his father must stay together."

The Lorenzanas left the Mission and rode south to Rancho del Mar. At the ranch house Doña Francisca greeted Sebastián and Moisés with warmth and gentle kindness. She was upset to see how miserable they looked. Don José put Tomás in charge of Sebastián while Beatriz took Moisés from Anita.

"Come into the kitchen with me," said Doña Francisca to Beatriz. They looked at each other sadly as they saw how pitifully thin Moisés had become. "He's so starved he has no strength to cry," whispered Doña Francisca. "Let's give him a little milk and boiled water. Not much. We'll give him more later."

"We'll save him," said Beatriz firmly.

A short time later Moisés was fed, warmly wrapped and placed in the cradle in the kitchen where Beatriz could keep an eye on him.

"The color is coming back to his cheeks, Mother," exclaimed Anita. "He looks better already."

Outside on the porch Sebastián drank more soup and watched Moisés through the kitchen door. Then Tomás brought Sebastián to a small storage room off the courtyard where Sebastián lay down to sleep under a wool blanket on a bed of soft sheepskins.

A few days later everyone woke up at the crack of dawn. With strong healthy lungs, Moisés was yelling for breakfast at daylight. Nobody minded being waked so early. They knew Moisés was getting well. That same day Sebastián left his bed and sat in the sunlight braiding a new leather lariat for Don José.

Within four weeks Moisés started climbing out of the cradle and scooting around the floor on hands and knees. He crawled all over Old Brownie, the ranch dog, who suffered the indignity of being sat on, having his long ears pulled and his tail grabbed. When Moisés pulled over the bean barrel, Beatriz called for help.

"Tomás, what can I do? Tie him up? I'm afraid he'll pull a pot of hot water over on himself."

Tomás' tanned face creased into one of his rare smiles. "We need a baby corral," he said. That day a small section of the patio was fenced off from the courtyard. They settled Moisés in the little pen with a supply of small rattles, a throwing stick and other toys.

Wise Old Brownie elected to stand guard, out of reach, by the gate of the baby corral. El Duque and La Reina Victoria learned to distance themselves from the baby's investigating fingers, but one day the toddler grabbed Victoria's fluffy tail. She scratched his arm. Moisés cried for Sebastián who cut a leaf from the aloe plant and squeezed its healing sap on the scratch.

Each time someone passed by the baby corral, Moisés would call out a greeting that sounded like "Yoo hoo!" Everybody from Don José to the youngest *vaquero* was expected to respond. If someone forgot to greet him, he would protest loudly in Chumash baby talk. He scolded until the offender came over and talked to him.

"Do you have a smile for your godmother today?" Anita always tickled him under his chin to make him laugh.

"Hello, Moisés," Don José would say.

"How are you today, *compadre?*" Pedro would ask.

Moisés liked to perch on Sebastián's shoulders for a piggy back ride around the courtyard. Soon Tomás was holding him on the pommel of the saddle and riding around the ranch with him. Like a true *vaquero* Moisés could ride before he could walk. He had become part of the family of Rancho del Mar.

12

IN THE WRONG PLACE
AT THE RIGHT TIME

Most satisfactory." Don José nodded his approval as Mr. O'Leary inked in the finishing touches on a map of the land *comisión*. "An excellent copy of the *diseño* to use when Mr. Prescott surveys our rancho."

"Just a few more details to add," replied Mr. O'Leary. It had been an exacting job to draw freehand a neat copy of the original map. "Anita, would you please hand me that blue pen?"

"When you finish," said Don José, "put the new map and the other land title papers in my leather case. Give it to Francisca. She knows where I keep them. I'm riding off now with Tomás to inspect a spring that seems to have gone dry. Lorenzo, Tonio and Fernando have gone on an overnight hunting trip. Sebastián and Moisés are with them."

"Don't worry. I'll take care of everything." Mr. O'Leary dipped his pen in the inkwell. He was drawing the last curve of the Santa Clara riverbed when María Isabel entered the room.

"How did I do on my geometry test?" María Isabel wanted to know.

"A perfect paper." Mr. O'Leary smiled into her dark eyes.

"And my division problems?" asked Anita with an anxious look.

"Excellent as always." The tutor answered with a soft voice. After concentrating so long and hard on mapmaking, the presence of María Isabel changed his mood from serious to playful. He laughed, took out a stick of red sealing wax from his desk and struck a match to light the candle. He melted the end of the stick in the flame, dripped a little of the hot sealing wax on each test paper and pressed his signet ring in the red wax. "There. My *rúbrica* makes it legal." Mr. O'Leary signed his name on each test paper with an elaborate series of loops, circles and zigzag lines. "Signed, sealed and delivered."

The girls admired the intricate flourishes that made his signature different from any other. "Mr. O'Leary, it's time for my English lesson," María Isabel reminded him.

"We can go outside and sit in the shade under the *ramada*. First I must put the maps away in their case and give it to Doña Francisca. Then I'll gather up all the mathematics papers and put them away in my desk."

"I can do that for you," offered Anita. Her hands picked up the maps and slipped them into the case while her eyes watched Mr. O'Leary. An amused smile turned up the corners of her mouth. He's so transparent, she thought. He's head over heels in love with María Isabel. While inserting the pile of mathematics papers in the other leather case, she watched through the doorway as Mr. O'Leary sat down beside her sister in the shade.

Anita put Mr. O'Leary's case in the top drawer of his desk and took her father's case to Doña Francisca. She found her mother sewing a complicated seam on a dress. Doña Francisca frowned slightly at the interruption. She sighed and put down her work. Anita watched as her mother placed the case in a secret compartment Don José had built behind a wall panel. Doña Francisca returned immediately to her chair, picked up her needle, and bent over the difficult seam.

Anita went into her room and lay down for a siesta. When she awoke, the late afternoon sun hung like a golden globe in the western sky. In the quiet dreamy twilight between darkness and daylight, time seemed to stand still.

Each member of the family remaining at home was busy with his own affairs. Tía Luisa sat on the balcony taking advantage of the last rays of sunlight to work a few more stitches on an embroidered collar. El Duque dozed beside her on the railing. Doña Francisca and Beatriz were checking supplies in the kitchen. The maids were busy folding clothes in the storeroom. Anita sat down on the bench outside the kitchen door waiting for her father to come home. Not far away Pedro, the young *vaquero,* stood by the *ramada* coiling a leather lariat he had just mended. On the other side of the east wall Anita could hear Mr. O'Leary and María Isabel talking about two rose bushes that needed pruning.

"They haven't been doing well this year," said María Isabel.

Mr. O'Leary whacked at a weed with his sturdy black-thorn walking stick and said, "The roses need to be cut here, and here, and here to encourage new growth." Their footsteps faded away toward the cornfield.

Three rough looking riders burst into the courtyard at full gallop. The leader rode straight to the porch and reined in sharply in front of Anita. He stopped directly under the balcony railing where El Duque crouched. Drawing their pistols, the other two outlaws dismounted and took positions on either side of the leader. One man waved his pistol at Pedro who stood perfectly still, his lariat in his hands. From the balcony Tía Luisa shrieked, *"Bandidos! Bandidos!"*

The leader aimed his pistol at Anita. "Where are the title papers to the ranch? Quick, tell me or I'll shoot." A fluffy feather in his hatband bounced with each word he said.

Anita felt helpless, so paralyzed with fright she couldn't move. She stared at the black hole at the end of the pistol barrel like a bird hypnotized by a snake. This must be how Father felt, she thought. Is this bandit really going to shoot me?

Doña Francisca, followed closely by Beatriz, rushed out through the kitchen door. Facing the bandit, she stood in front of Anita and stretched out her arms to shield her daughter. "What is it? What do you want?" she cried.

"Give me the papers to Rancho del Mar," the man demanded.

"We don't have any papers here." Doña Francisca's voice was unsteady. She feared for Anita.

"Señora, we know that you keep the commission papers of the *rancho* in a secret place in your house. Don't play games with me. Bring them here at once, or I shoot the girl."

"Don't you dare speak to my mother like that." Anita cried out. Her eyes blazed. She felt frightened and angry at the same time.

"You, Rábano, go with the *señora* and get the papers. I'll keep this little spitfire under control. Sánchez, keep your eye on the *vaquero*.

Pale and shaking, Doña Francisca led the bandit, Rábano, to the sewing room where the leather case was locked in the secret compartment.

On the other side of the courtyard wall Mr. O'Leary and María Isabel had heard Tía Luisa's shriek and the bandit leader's loud voice. The tutor gave María Isabel a gentle push. "Quick, run and hide in the cornfield," he ordered. She ran.

Mr. O'Leary hurried to the gateway, paused a second, and then entered the courtyard as if he were coming on stage. Leaning on his blackthorn stick, he hobbled over to the outlaws like a frail and feeble invalid. "What's the matter?" he asked in a quavering voice.

"Get over here and don't do anything stupid," Sánchez growled.

Mr. O'Leary hobbled over to him and stood within reach of the hand that held the pistol. Over by the *ramada*, his lariat coiled in his hands, Pedro watched the bandits with wary eyes.

"I've got them, Espina. Here they are," yelled Rábano running outside. He opened the case and waved the white papers at the bandit chief.

Crouched on the railing above, El Duque had taken an immense dislike to that fluffy bobbing feather. He arched his back and hissed, glaring down at the hateful thing. Then everything happened at once.

Whomph! With an earsplitting caterwauling screech,

six pounds of cat landed on the bandit leader's head. The hat with its offensive feather fell to the ground. As El Duque leaped after it, his sharp claws raked the hindquarters of the leader's horse. The horse bucked and threw Espina face down in the dust where he dropped his pistol.

Before he could get up, Beatriz sat on him and gently touched his ear lobe with the sharp tip of her skinning knife. "Don't move," she said in a grim voice.

At the same instant, Mr. O'Leary brought down his blackthorn stick hard on Sánchez' arm. Sánchez dropped his pistol and cried out in pain. Gripping the case with its precious contents, Rábano jumped into his saddle and spurred his horse through the gateway. A few white papers fluttered to the ground behind him.

His arm dangling, Sánchez leaped on his horse and wheeled about to follow Rábano. Quick as a flash Pedro threw his lariat, caught Sánchez around the waist and pulled him to the ground. His frightened mount streaked through the gateway behind the other horses.

On the hard-packed earth of the courtyard, El Duque attacked the fluffy feather like a fox chasing a chicken. In one minute, thanks to him, everything was over.

Always level headed in a crisis Doña Francisca spoke calmly to Anita. "Go over to the corral fence and bring back the lariat hanging there."

The bandit leader was deathly afraid of Beatriz. "Get her off me," he begged, coughing in the dust. Pedro tied his hands and feet while Mr. O'Leary pointed Espina's pistol at Sánchez. Tía Luisa did not want to miss any of the excitement. She ran down the balcony stairs eager to take part in the capture. After the two bandits were safely tied up, Mr. O'Leary handed the pistol to Tía Luisa. He stepped into the storeroom to reassure the frightened maids and hurried back to the cornfield to find María Isabel.

Anita heard the drumbeat of hoofs and Brownie's joyful bark outside the south wall. In the gathering darkness Don José and Tomás rode through the gateway, leading two saddled and riderless horses. The *ranchero's* eyes widened as he saw the two men trussed up on the ground, his sister holding a pistol, and his wife on the porch bench holding her head. María Isabel and Mr. O'Leary were sitting beside her.

"What's going on here?" demanded Don José.

Brownie ran forward and crouched by Espina. A menacing growl rose from the ranch dog's throat.

"Everything is all right now, Father," said Anita as she picked up a fluttering sheet of paper. "Mr. O'Leary saved us from the robbers."

"Ah, no. It was that fine black cat of yours who saved us, sir. He jumped on the leader's head, and his horse bucked and threw him on the ground. I was lucky and hit one of the *spalpeens* with my blackthorn stick. Then Pedro lassoed him when he tried to get away," explained Mr. O'Leary who had forgotten that he was still holding María Isabel by the hand.

"José!" Doña Francisca sobbed. "One man got away with the title papers to the ranch. I had to give them up. He would have shot Anita."

Don José hurried to his wife and held her in his arms. He exhaled a deep breath. "At least none of you is hurt."

He turned to Espina and asked in an icy voice, "Who sent you here?"

Espina shook his head and refused to answer. Beatriz gently nicked his ear lobe with her sharp knife. "Answer the *dueño*," she ordered.

Don José repeated his question. Again the bandit shook

his head. Beatriz moved the knife to his chin. Brownie snarled and growled louder.

"I'll tell. I'll tell. It was Señor Teodoro Valencia."

"I suspected him from the beginning, but I had no proof. He's the one who has been trying to ruin us and take over our *rancho*." Don José's jaw set. He pulled his pistol from his belt and checked the barrel. "I'll make sure he doesn't try to harm my family again!"

"José, what are you planning to do?" Doña Francisca held his arm in a tight grip.

"I'm going to go to see him and get the papers back."

"Sir," said Mr. O'Leary, "wouldn't it be better to wait until daylight and take your vaqueros —"

"No. It's a matter of personal honor. He'll face my pistol before daylight."

"José, I'm going with you. This is a matter of Toral honor, too."

"No! Absolutely not! I forbid it. It's my duty, not yours."

Doña Francisca looked straight into his eyes. "Have you forgotten I am a *comandante's* daughter?" Her gentle voice was resolute. "Where you go, I go."

"Mother! Father! Stop!" Anita was holding a sheet of paper to the light streaming from the kitchen doorway. "They didn't steal the title papers. Look!"

Don José strode to Anita's side and took the white sheets from her hand. He examined them in the light. "These are geometry tests. I don't understand. What are you talking about? Where are the papers?"

Anita ran inside the *sala* to Mr. O'Leary's desk and came out with a leather case. "Right here. I put them in the wrong case by mistake. The case the bandit stole was full of geometry papers."

She handed the case to her father and burst out laughing.

She laughed so hard she had to wipe the tears from her eyes. "Can't you just see Señor Valencia in his *sala* lounging by his copper *brasero*, toasting his toes and drinking his chocolate? Then that bandit comes in and hands over the papers with line drawings, numbers, red seals and official looking rubric signatures. All Señor Valencia has for his scheming is a packet of geometry tests!

The bandit leader snarled and spit dust from his mouth. "Are you telling me the whole plan failed because Rábano couldn't read?"

"You threatened to shoot my daughter and bullied my wife and that's all you have to say?" Don José's voice roared in anger.

For a second Anita thought her father would kick the bandit in the ribs, but with great effort Don José controlled himself.

"You two outlaws will face Captain Noriega tomorrow. He'll send you in chains to the captain of the *Vindicta* for deportation to the prison in Acapulco. Believe me, that captain and his crew will not take kindly to a coward who threatened to shoot a twelve-year-old girl.

"I'll bring that *villano* Valencia to justice before the Santa Barbara District Council. They will ask him some hard questions. I doubt he will have straight answers." His hands shaking with suppressed rage, Don José removed the silver spurs from his boots, dropped them on the bench and strode toward the *sala* followed by Doña Francisca.

Anita stroked El Duque's glistening black coat. "We couldn't have done it without you, you beautiful, precious, wonderful cat."

El Duque accepted Anita's praise with feline dignity. He rubbed against Tía Luisa's skirt and purred as she promised him a nice piece of chicken liver for dinner. He allowed Mr.

O'Leary and María Isabel to scratch his head behind his ears. Then he yawned and stretched and stalked haughtily away like his namesake, the royal duke of Alba. It was time to attend to serious business. When all was said and done, there were still mice to catch and a gopher hole to watch.

EPILOGUE

*A*nita **walked over** to the corral fence where Mr. O'Leary was talking to El Cid in a low voice. "Would you like to ride to the ocean with me, Mr. O'Leary?" she asked. "Tonio is helping Fernando this afternoon and I'm not allowed to ride alone."

"El Cid and I would enjoy that," said Mr. O'Leary.

"I'll be ready in a few minutes," replied Anita. She hurried across the courtyard and up the stairs. On the second floor she met María Isabel who watched from the balcony as a *vaquero* led out El Cid and Chocolate.

"Are you going for a ride?" asked María Isabel. "I think I'll go along, too."

"Hurry up. Tell the *vaquero* to saddle another horse." The sisters used to ride often together, but when María Isabel was about fifteen, she had become more interested in boys and fiestas and never seemed to have time to ride.

Anita pulled on the old pair of Tonio's pants and the old flowered skirt she always wore when riding. She turned around to see María Isabel had changed to her new brown riding clothes. "That's a beautiful outfit," said Anita.

Her sister smiled, tucked a band around her hair and took down their broad brimmed hats from a peg on the wall. "Let's go," she said, handing Anita her hat.

Mr. O'Leary's face broke into a wide smile when he saw María Isabel coming. Anita mounted Chocolate, looked back and saw Mr. O'Leary helping her sister up on her horse. Hmph, thought Anita, suddenly she's so helpless she can't get in the saddle by herself.

Lying in the shade by the courtyard gate Brownie pricked up his ears, stood up, shook himself and trotted off after Chocolate. He knew they were headed toward the ocean. That meant he could have some fun chasing sea gulls.

Chocolate remembered how cool the water felt on his hoofs and fetlocks. He charged forward, eager to walk through the surf.

María Isabel and Mr. O'Leary lagged behind, deep in conversation. María Isabel began to teach Mr. O'Leary a song. He had a fine tenor voice.

"Like this, Maribel?" asked Mr. O'Leary singing a few bars.

"Yes, Edward, that's exactly right."

Hmm, said Anita to herself, so it's Maribel and Edward, is it? She never let anyone call her Maribel before. Very interesting. I wonder if Mother knows. I think I'll keep quiet about this and not tell anyone. Father might make Mr. O'Leary go away. I wouldn't want that. He helps Father in ways that none of us can.

So many things have happened this year. I feel much older somehow. Since Governor Chico left suddenly for Mexico, that *malvado*, Valencia, lost his political protection. Father brought him before the Santa Barbara District Council on charges of fraud and grievous assault. Rábano came out of hiding to testify against his former *dueño*. After testifying, Rábano was released and disappeared before El Malo could find him.

The council recommended to the Acting Governor Gutiérrez that Valencia be deported to Mexico as a criminal and forbidden to return to California. Gutiérrez signed the order. Valencia sold Rancho del Agua Dulce to Samuel Slope for a small sum. Those *bellacones*, the Santos brothers, will stay on at the ranch with Slope. Tía Luisa thinks they are plotting more trouble for us.

It all started when Don Ramón came to Mother's birthday party. Pedro's cousin, who works on Rancho del Agua Dulce, told Pedro that Don Ramón double-crossed Valencia. Don Ramón was supposed to steal the land commission papers to Rancho del Mar. Instead he stole the money, gave El Malo the slip and got clean away to Santa Barbara. Cecilia's brother said that the next day a man of Don Ramón's description boarded an American ship bound for Hong Kong. We can't prove anything though.

Chocolate began to run faster because he could smell the ocean and hear the surf. He galloped through a field of milkweed. Suddenly thousands of big orange and black butterflies floated up around them. One landed on his nostril and tickled him. He snorted indignantly.

"What's the matter Chocolate? Those are just monarch butterflies. They remind me of flying flowers," said Anita.

Chocolate felt it was all very well for Anita to talk about flying flowers, but that pesky flutterbye was tickling his nose, not her nose.

Brownie paid no attention to the butterflies. He ran to the beach where a flock of sea gulls rested on the sand in the sun, dreaming their sea gull dreams. He raced through the flock, scattering them right and left. Then he turned around barking and leaping up in the air as they took flight. They squawked and scolded him. At Anita's call, he returned obediently, his eyes shining with fun and his pink tongue lolling out of a doggy grin. "Good old Brownie," said Anita. "Tonio says that dogs can't laugh, but what does he know, eh, old fellow?"

Chocolate galloped over a sand dune. "Here's the ocean," said Anita. "You like that, don't you?" Chocolate tossed his head with pleasure, up to his fetlocks in the cool salt water.

Anita looked out to sea. She saw a familiar sight, an American brig about a mile offshore. Its sails billowed out in the wind and a long red and white homeward bound pennant streamed from the tall foremast. She stood up high in the stirrups and waved her hat in the air. The sunlight glinted off a brass spyglass. Then she saw a puff of smoke and heard the booming sound of the signal cannon on deck.

Mr. O'Leary and María Isabel galloped their horses across the sand and stopped alongside Anita. The cannon shot echoed across the valley from hill to hill.

"They see us! They are signaling!" cried Anita waving her hat wildly. "Aloha! Aloha!"

The *Pride of Nantucket* was on her way home.

Glossary

A

adiós *ah-Dyos* goodbye

adobe *ah-Dough-bay* sun dried clay brick

amor *ah-More* love

Ave María Puríssima *Ah-vay mah-Ree-ah poor-Iss-i-mah* Hail Mary most pure (Latin)

Ay, Chihuahua *Eye, she-Wah-wah* Wow!

aventada *Ah-vane-Tah-dah* roundup of wild horses

B

bandidos *bahn-Dee-dose* bandits, robbers

barbacoa *bar-bah-Ko-ah* barbecue

Barbaroja *bar-bah-Row-hah* Redbeard

barranca *bar-Rahn-ka* deep gully from rain water runoff

bellacón *bay-yah-Kone* rogue

buenos días *Bway-nos-Dee-ahs* good morning!

C

caporal *kah-pore-Ahl* head vaquero, foreman

carreta *kar-Ray-tah* cart with two large wooden wheels

chaparral *chah-pah-Rahl* wild bushy range plants

Chumash *Shoo-mahsh* California coastal Indian tribe

El Cid *el-Seed* Spanish knight of the Middle Ages

cilantro *see-Lahn-tro* coriander leaf, somewhat like parsley

compadre *comb-Pah-dray* friend, companion

conejo *ko-Nay-ho* rabbit

contra danza *Kone-tra Dahn-sah* dance, couples opposite each other

cuartel *kwar-Tel* soldiers' barracks

169

D
diseño *dee-Sane-yo* large drawing of a land grant
diablo *dee-Ah-blow* devil
Don, Doña *Dohn, Dohn-ya* informal courtesy title
dueño *Dway-nyo* land owner

F
fandango *fahn-Dahn-go* Spanish dance, its music
fiesta *fee-Ess-ta* party
flor de noche buena *Floor day No-chay-Bway-na* poinsettia
frijoles *free-Ho-lace* beans

G
gente de razón *Hen-tay day rahs-Sawhn* land owning class
of people

L
loma *Low-mah* cow's back

M
El Malo *el-Mah-low* the bad man
malvado *mahl-Vah-dough* wicked man
masa *Mahs-sah* wet wheat or corn meal for making tortillas
menudo *may-Noo-dough* meat stew
merienda *mare-Yen-dah* light meal, picnic
miau *Mee-Yow* meow
miu *mee-You* mew

N
Niña Ana *Neen-yah Ah-nah* Little Miss Anne

O
olé *oh-Lay* Hurray!
olla *Oy-yah* clay jar

P

padre *Pah-dray* father
patas arriba *Pah-ta ssa-Ree-bah* upside down
poncho *Pahn-cho* heavy wool blanket
pozole *paw-Sso-lay* stew
presidio *pray-seed-Yoh* center of government

Q

querido, querida *care-Ree-dough, care-Ree-dah* darling,
dear
Que será, será *kay sir-Ah, sir-Ah* whatever will be, will be.

R

ramada *rah-Mah-dah* brush covered shelter with open sides
ranchería *rahn-chay-Ree-yah* Chumash village
Rancho del Agua Dulce *Ran-cho del-Ah-gwa-Dool-say*
Sweetwater Ranch
real *ray-Ahl* Spanish coin
refresco *ray-Fress-ko* refreshing drink
reata *ray-Ah-tah* lariat, braided leather or horsehair rope
rúbrica *Roo-bree-kah* elaborate signature

S

sala *Sah-lah* living room
salsa *Sahl-sah* tomato, onion and chile relish
sal si puedes *Sahl see Pway-dayss* go out if you can
Señor, Señora *sayn-Yor, sayn-Yor-ah* Mr., Mrs.
serape *say-Rah-pay* wool blanket that goes on over head

T

Tía Luisa *Tee-ah loo-Ee-sah* Aunt Louise
tortilla *tore-Tee-yah* thin pancake of wheat or corn meal

V

vaquero *vah-Kay-row* buckaroo, cowboy
villano *vee-Yah-no* villain, contemptible person

About the Author.

Elaine F. O'Brien, married to a naval officer/electronic engineer, holds degrees from Columbia and Stanford Universities and has studied at the University of Valencia, Spain. The missions and ranchos of California have held a special charm for her since she first came to California. She taught Spanish at Ventura High School and has served as Docent at the Ventura County Museum of History and Art since 1981. Currently she and her husband live on the land of the fictional Rancho del Mar, not far from the Olivas Adobe, the inspiration and model for the ranch house of the story.